Sports Illustrated KIDS

GRAPHIC NOVELS

STONE ARCH BOOKS
a capstone imprint

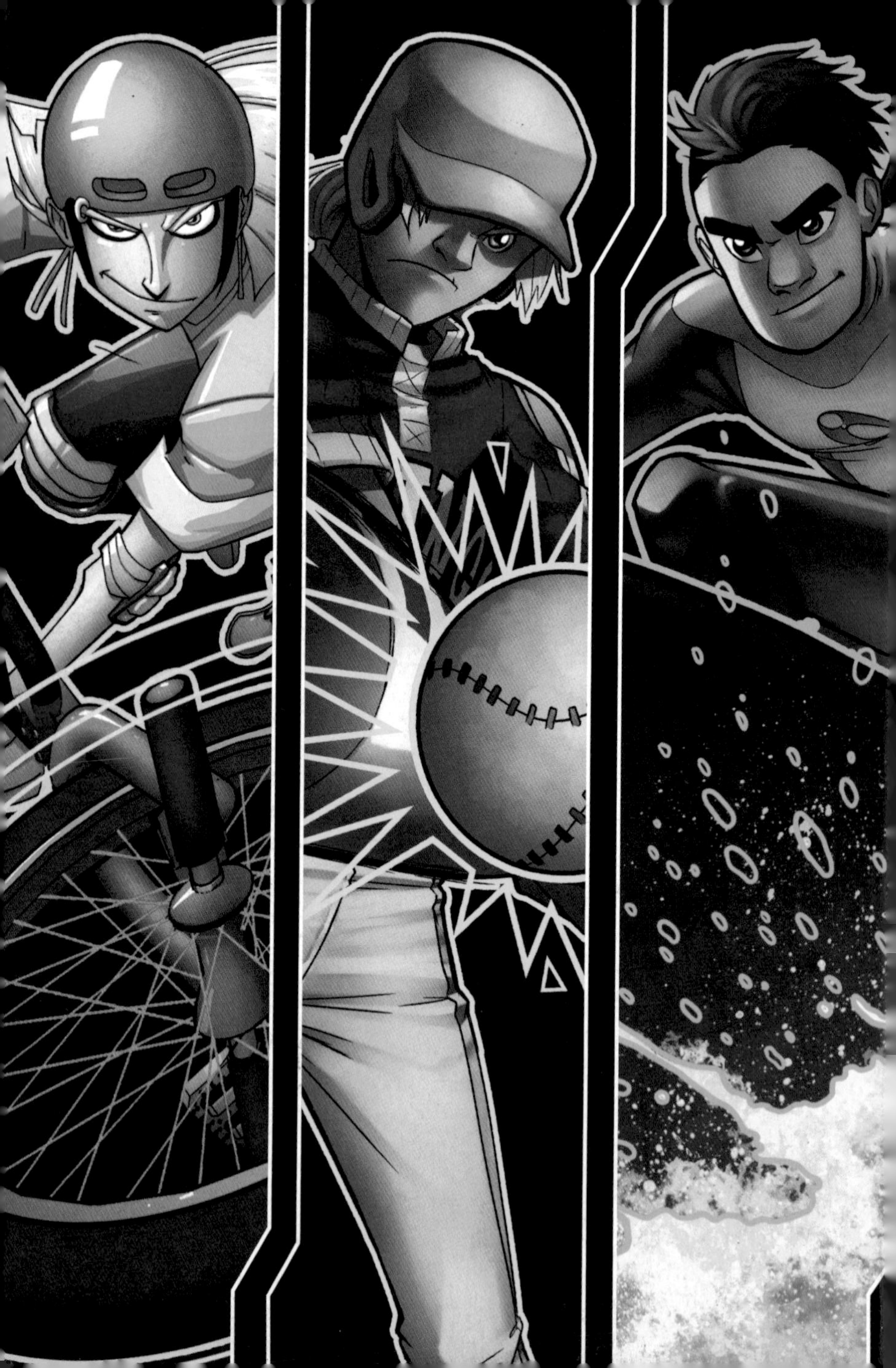

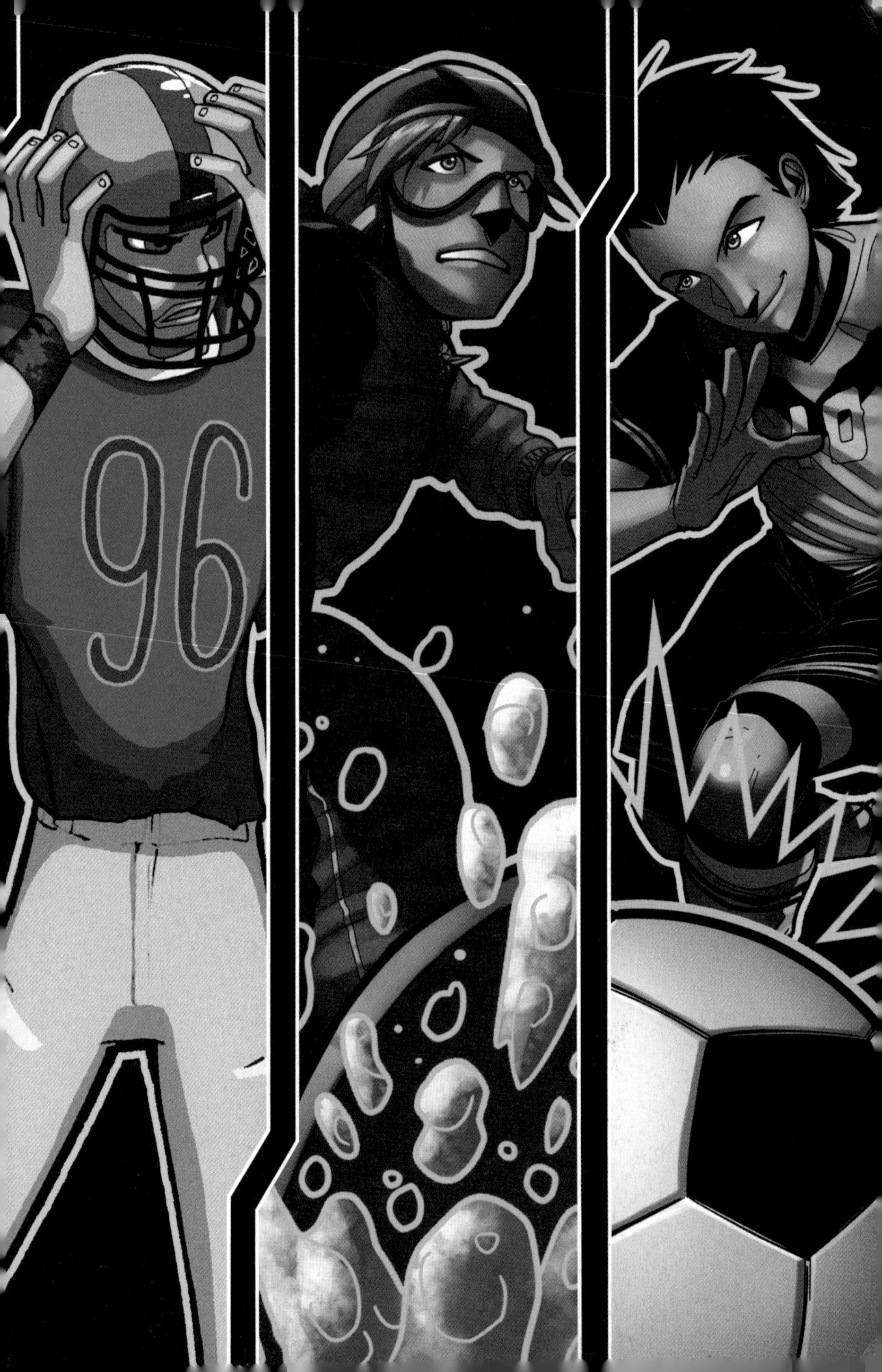

UP NEXT ›››

on Sports Illustrated KIDS

:02 SPORTS ZONE SPECIAL REPORT

:04 FEATURE PRESENTATION:

SOCCER LONGSHOT

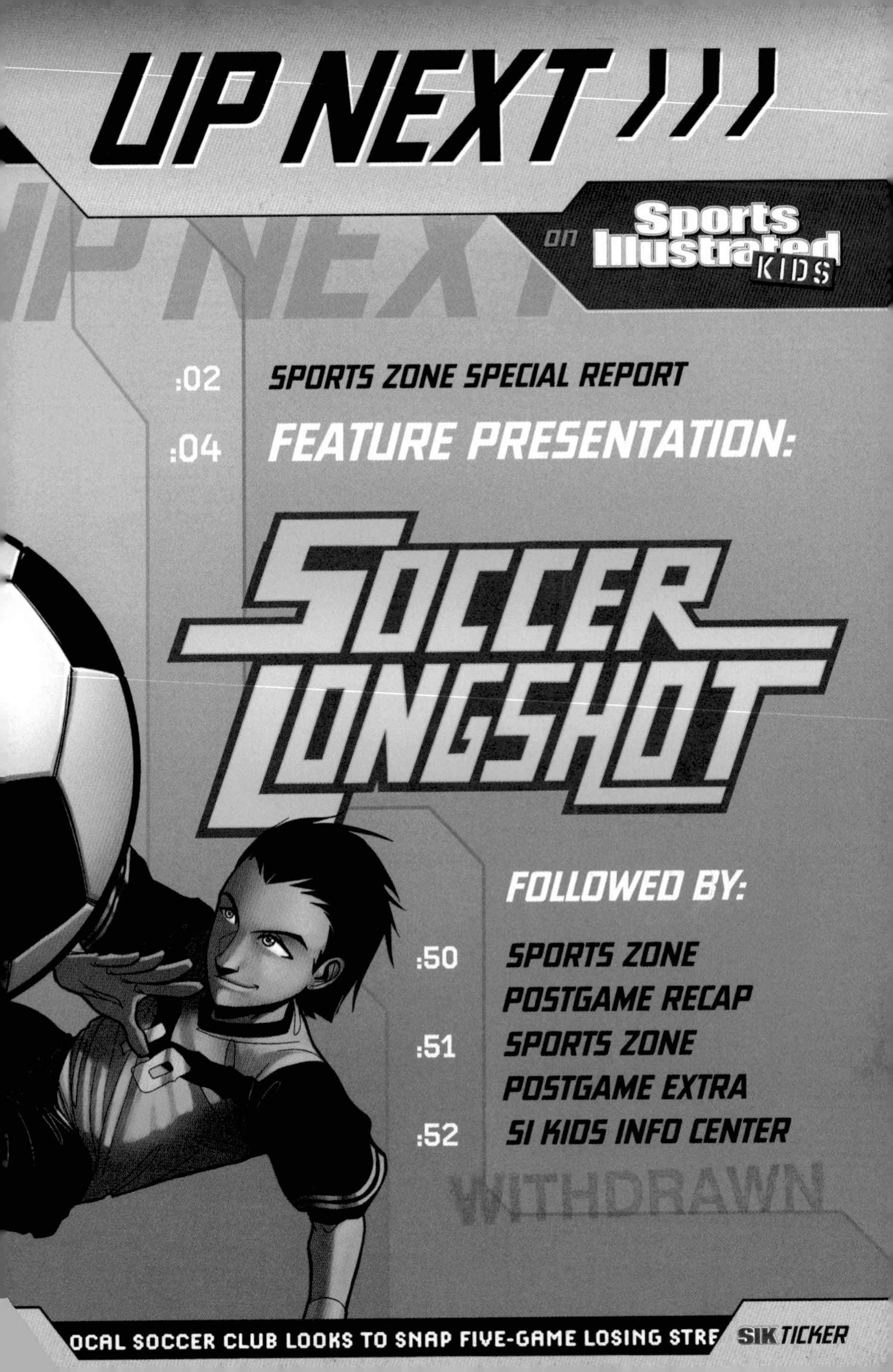

FOLLOWED BY:

:50 SPORTS ZONE POSTGAME RECAP

:51 SPORTS ZONE POSTGAME EXTRA

:52 SI KIDS INFO CENTER

OCAL SOCCER CLUB LOOKS TO SNAP FIVE-GAME LOSING STRE SIK TICKER

PORTS ZONE

IAL REPORT

SOCCER CLUB STAR SEEKS NEW CHALLENGES

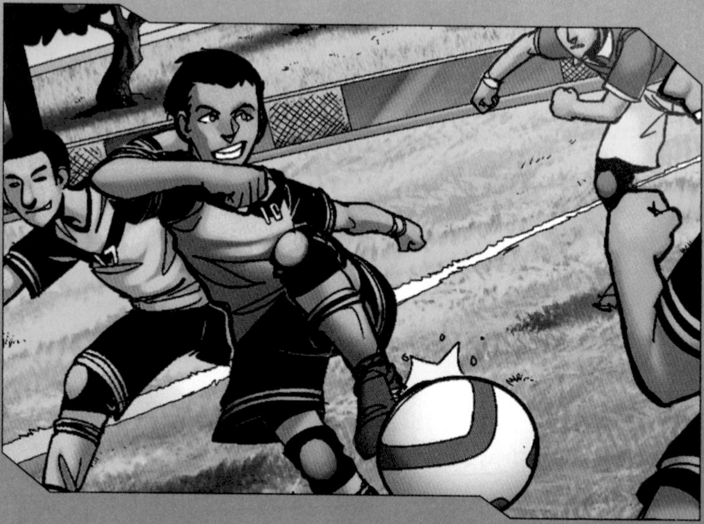

MATTY DRAKE

STATS:
AGE: 14
POSITION: FORWARD

BIO: Local soccer star Matty Drake has always been a gifted player, but lately he can't seem to shake the feeling that he hasn't improved in a while. In order to get out of his soccer rut, Matty will need to change things up and try something new — like, perhaps, the ratty field where the local streetball kids like to play...

UP NEXT: SOCCER LONGSHOT

LOLA NADIR

AGE: 14

POSITION: STRIKER

BIO: Lola loves the striker position. She's gifted at moving the ball and has a knack for getting lots of shots on goal. Of all the streetballers, she's the most skilled — and the most intense. The other players look up to her and treat her like a team captain.

BLZ vs BKS
3-1
TGR vs RO
33-32
EAG vs BA
14-7
SPA vs WI
4-3
BAN vs RO
21-15
RZR vs LIG
4-3
BLZ vs BKS

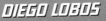

COACH LEWIS

AGE: 37

BIO: Coach Lewis is all about intensity. He believes that his players should play hard and with emotion, or not play at all.

DIEGO LOBOS

AGE: 14   POSITION: MIDFIELDER

BIO: Diego loves to set up Lola with shots on goal. He's always at the top of the team in assists and has a knack for flashy passes.

PHIL CARDIN

AGE: 14   POSITION: MIDFIELDER

BIO: Phil's a reliable player who shares the ball. He has top-notch defensive skills.

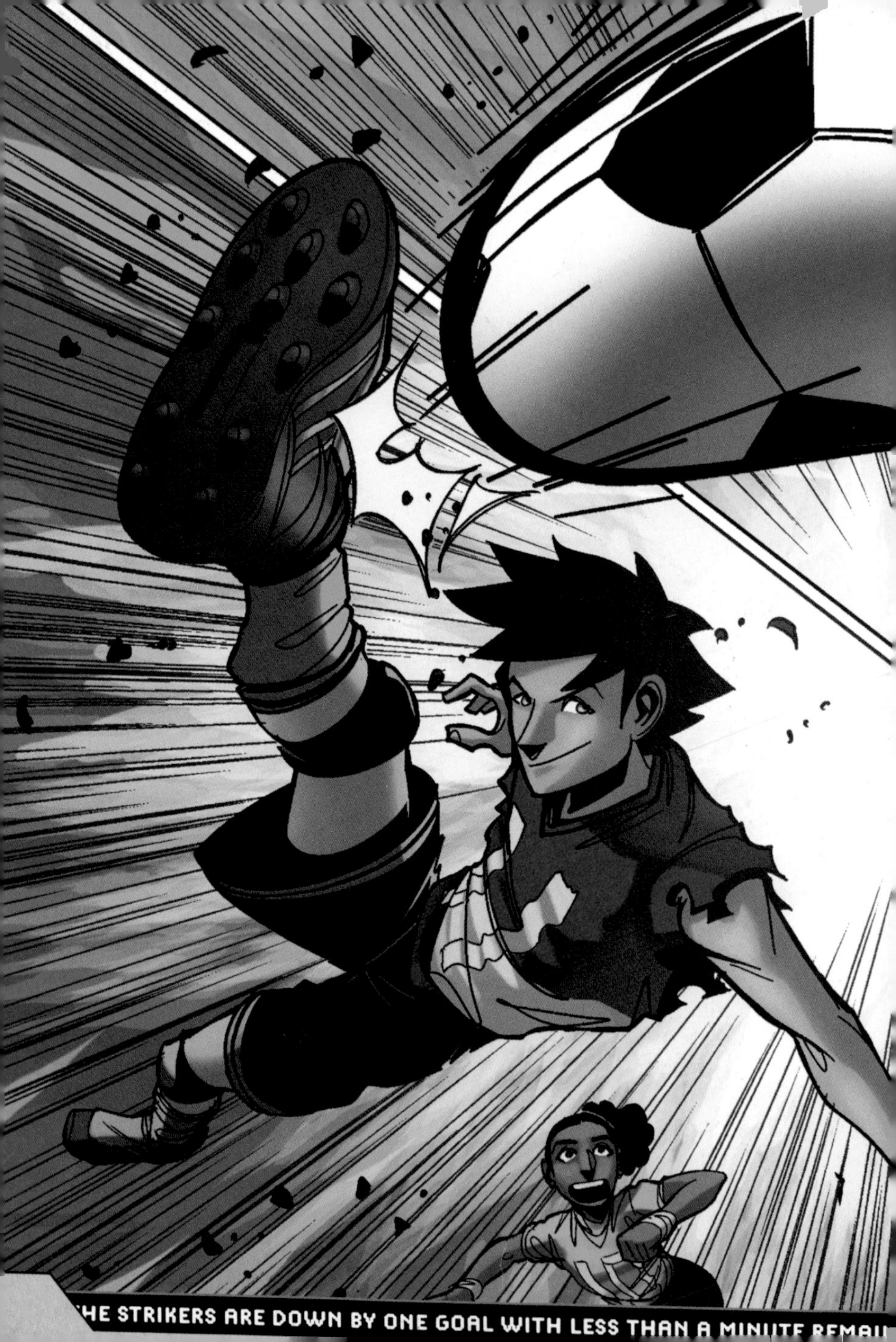
THE STRIKERS ARE DOWN BY ONE GOAL WITH LESS THAN A MINUTE REMAI

Sports Illustrated KIDS

PRESENTS

SOCCER LONGSHOT

A PRODUCTION OF

STONE ARCH BOOKS
a capstone imprint

written by C.J. Renner
penciled by Aburtov
inked by Andres Esparza
colored by Fernando Cano

designed and directed by Bob Lentz
edited by Sean Tulien
editorial management by Donald Lemke
creative direction by Heather Kindseth
editorial direction by Michael Dahl

Sports Illustrated KIDS *Soccer Longshot* is published by Stone Arch Books, 1710 Roe Crest Drive, North Mankato, Minnesota 56003.
www.capstonepub.com

Printed in the United States of America in Stevens Point, Wisconsin.
062015 009066R

Summary: Matty is the team captain of the local soccer club, the Strikers. His team is talented, but Matty can't help but feel that something's missing. He hasn't improved in a while, and wonders if he needs to switch things up in order to get better. So, he decides to head out to the local park to kick it with some of the street ball kids. Matty figures he'll run right through the disorganized teens. Instead, he gets a swift kick in the pants!

Library of Congress Cataloging-in-Publication Data
Renner, C. J.
Soccer longshot / written by C.J. Renner ; illustrated by Aburtov, Andres Esparza, and Fernando Cano.
p. cm. -- (Sports illustrated kids graphic novels)
ISBN 978-1-4342-2241-1 (library binding) -- ISBN 978-1-4342-3402-5 (pbk.)
1. Soccer stories. 2. Graphic novels. [1. Graphic novels. 2. Soccer--Fiction.] I. Aburtov, ill. II. Esparza, Andres, ill. III. Cano, Fernando, ill. IV. Title. V. Series: Sports illustrated kids graphic novels.
PZ7.7.R47So 2012
741.5'973--dc22 2011008314

ATTY DRAKE HAS BEEN SHUT OUT FOR THE FIRST TIME ALL SEASO SIK TICKER

With time winding down, the Strikers need to make something happen soon!
Matty has stolen the ball!
FWIP!

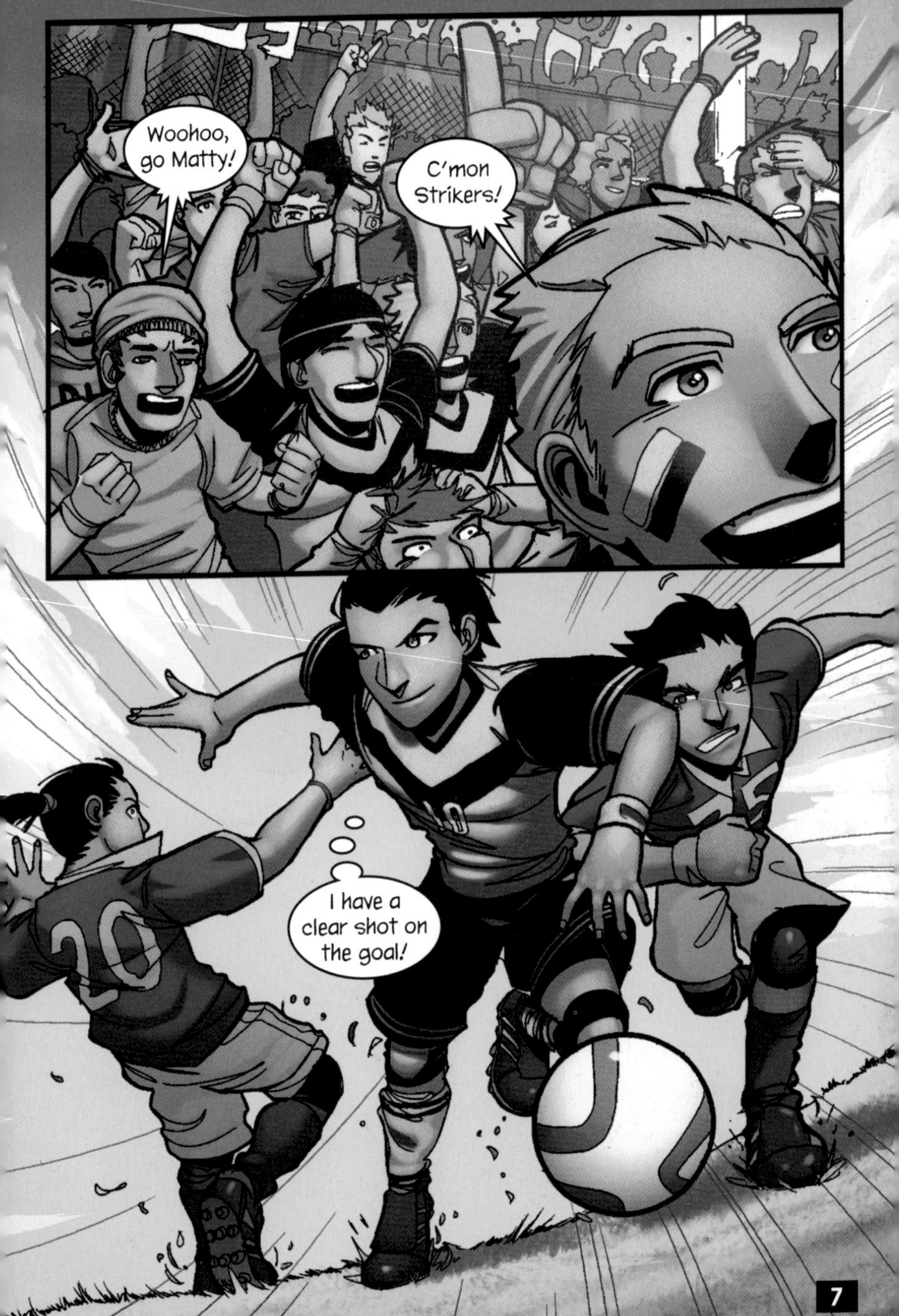
Woohoo, go Matty!
C'mon Strikers!
I have a clear shot on the goal!

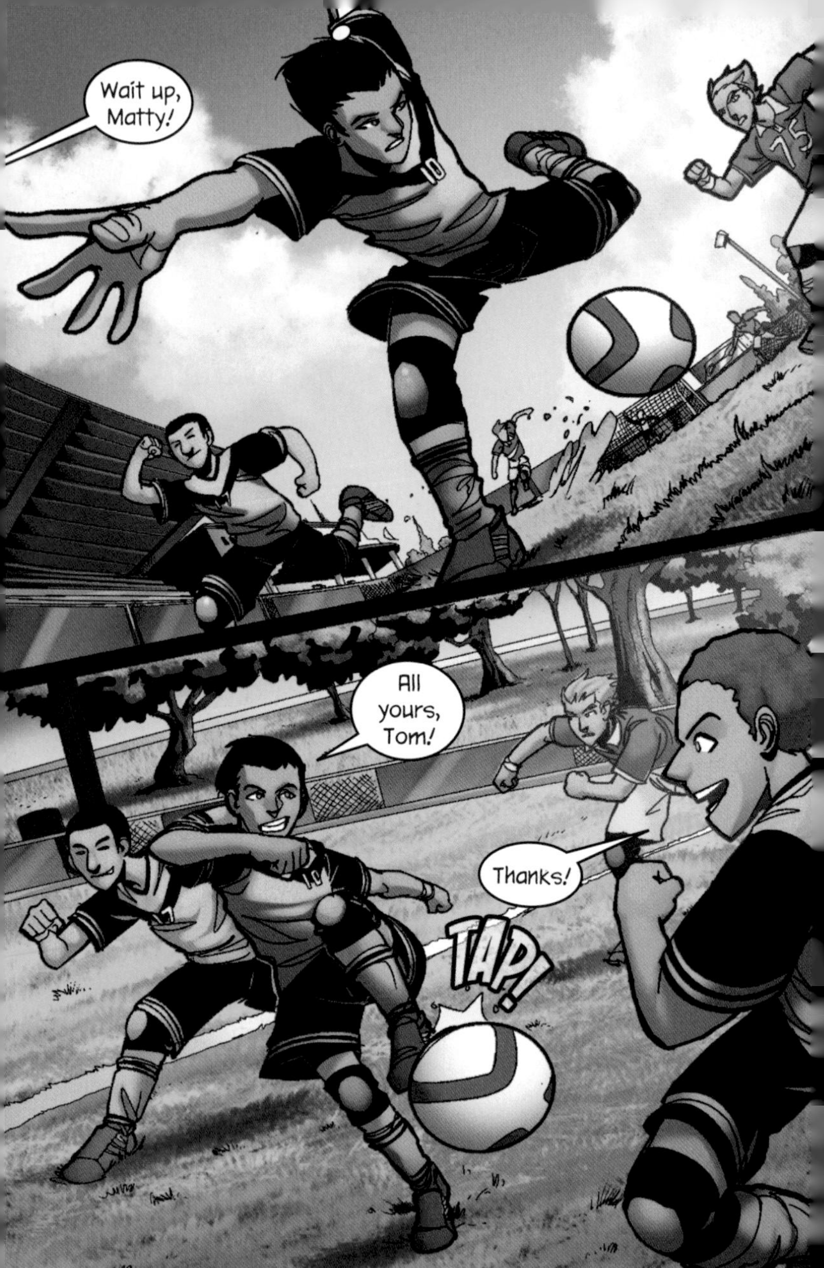
Wait up, Matty!
All yours, Tom!
Thanks!
TAP!

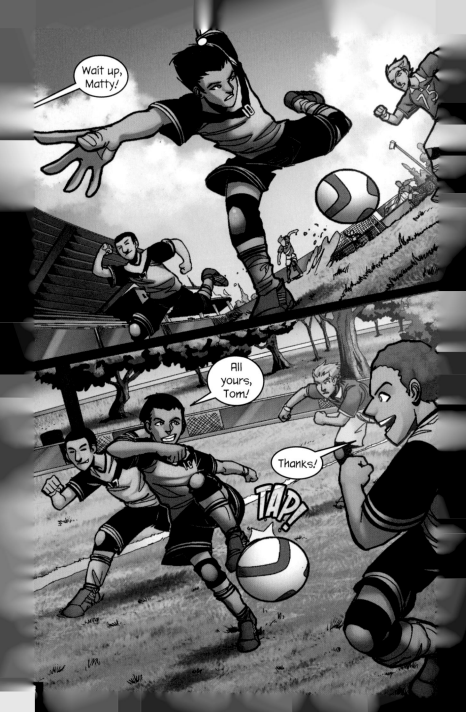

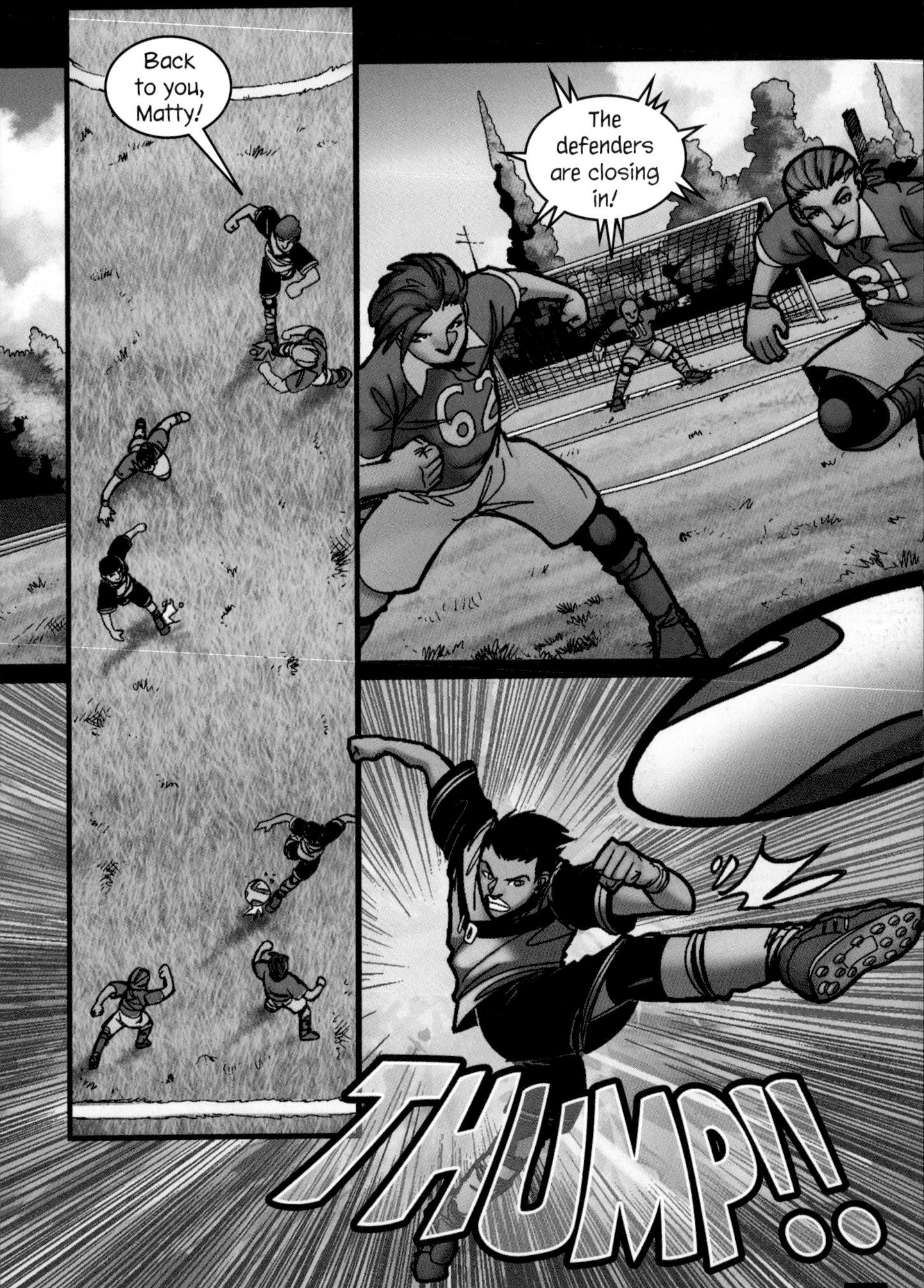
Back to you, Matty!
The defenders are closing in!
THUMP!!

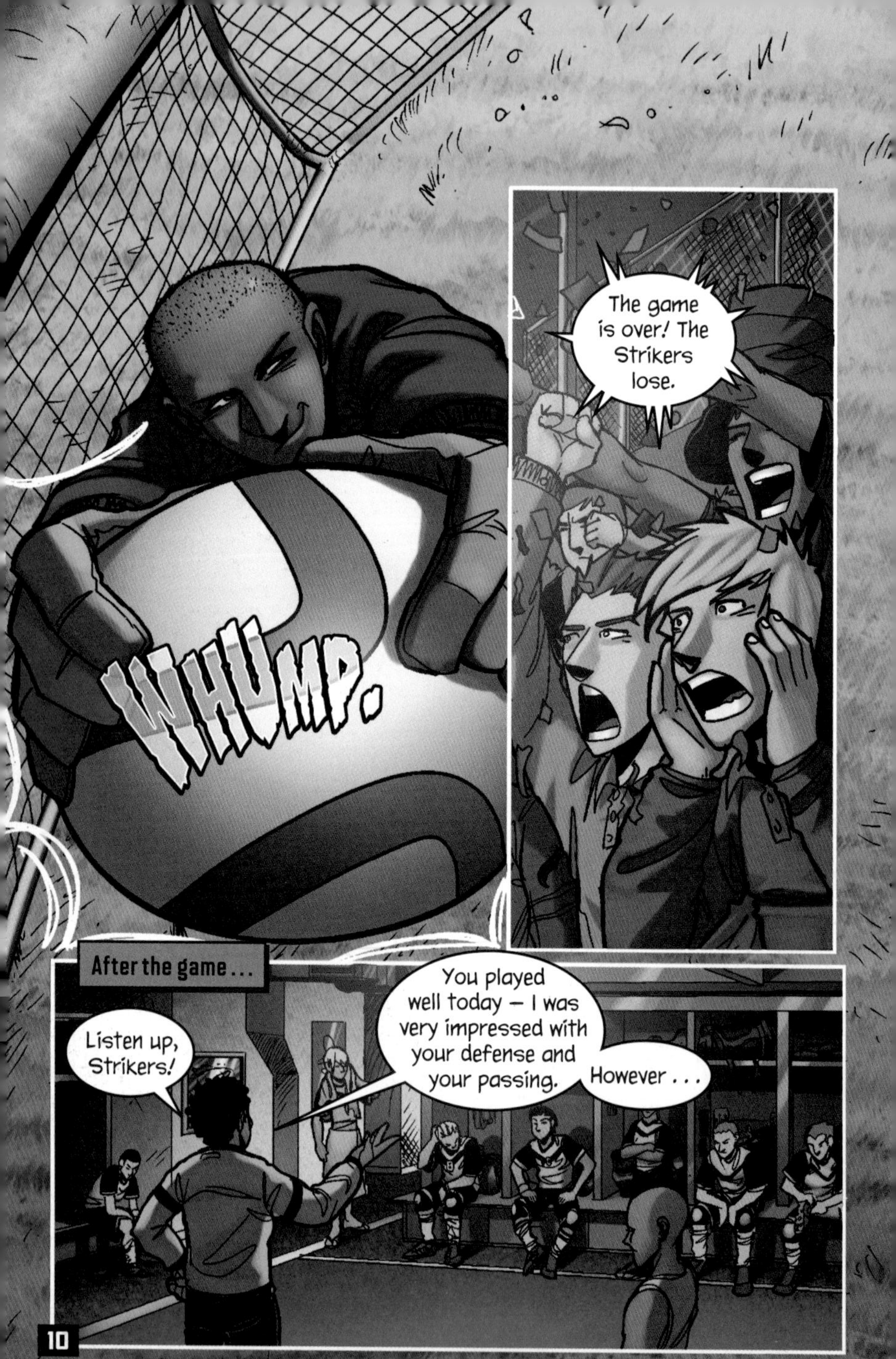
WHUMP.
The game is over! The Strikers lose.
After the game . . .
Listen up, Strikers!
You played well today — I was very impressed with your defense and your passing.
However . . .

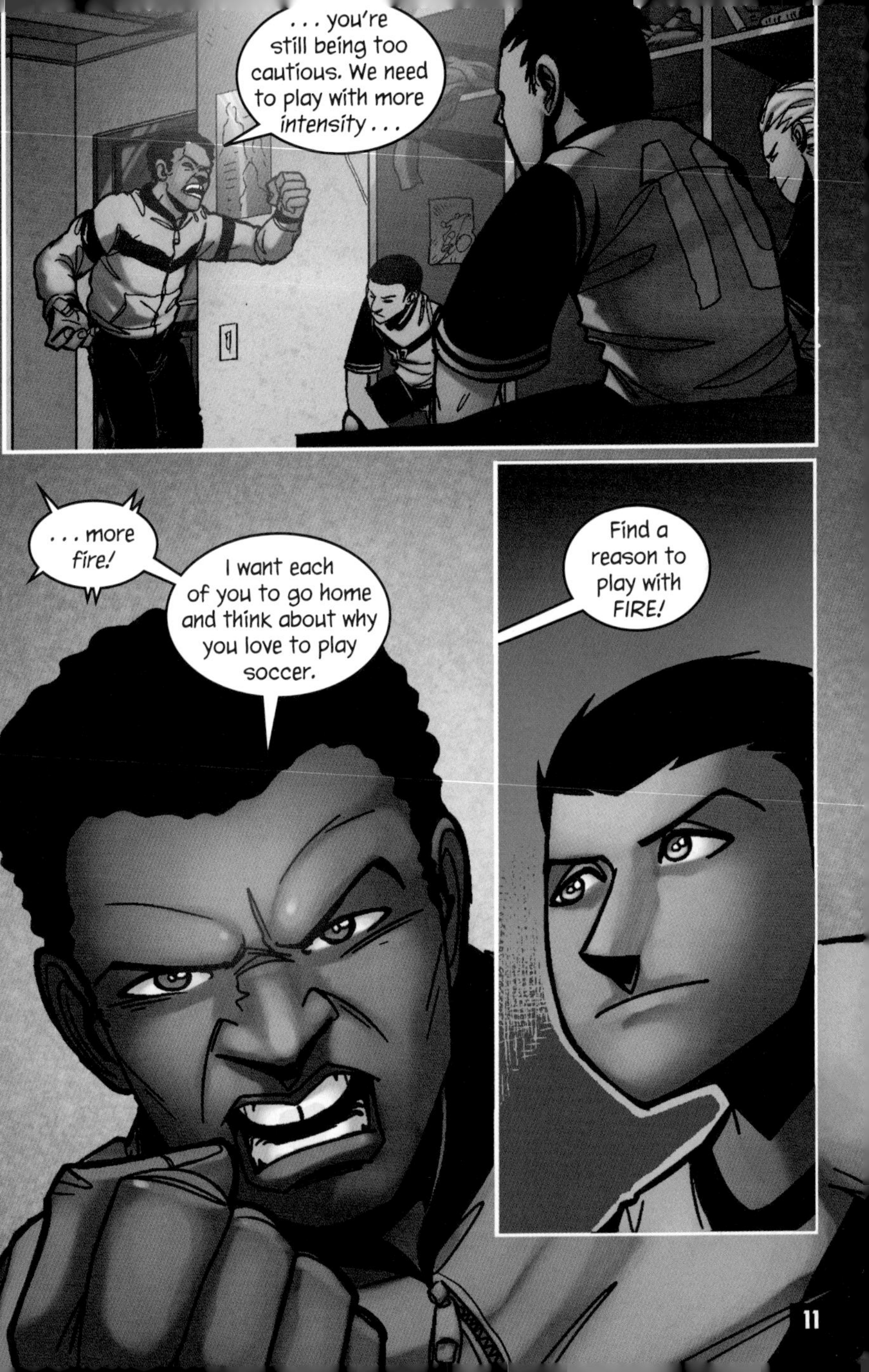
. . . you're still being too cautious. We need to play with more intensity . . .
. . . more fire!
I want each of you to go home and think about why you love to play soccer.
Find a reason to play with FIRE!

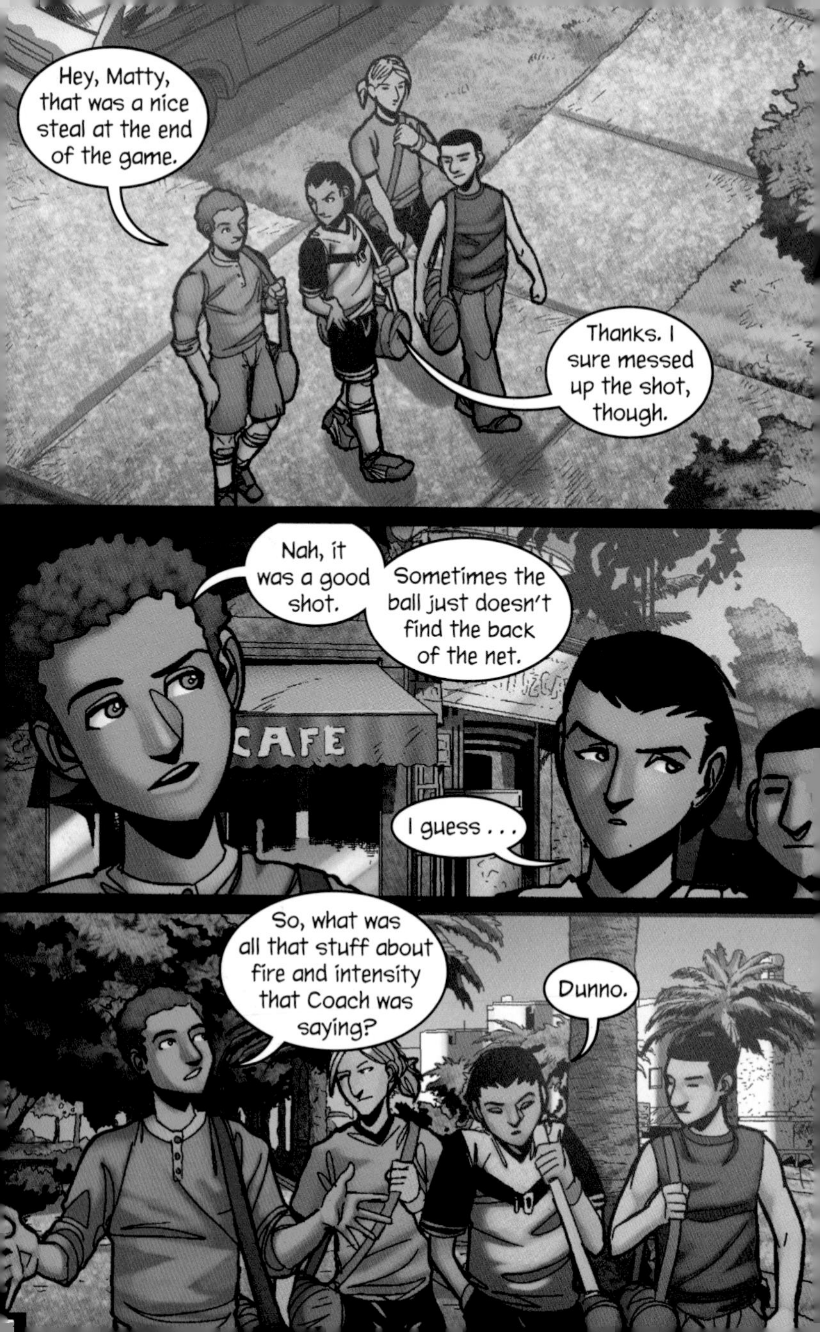
Hey, Matty, that was a nice steal at the end of the game.
Thanks. I sure messed up the shot, though.
Nah, it was a good shot.
Sometimes the ball just doesn't find the back of the net.
CAFE
I guess . . .
So, what was all that stuff about fire and intensity that Coach was saying?
Dunno.

Maybe he meant we should eat some hot sauce before games. That'd heat you up fast!
TACO DON PEPE
Or a whole bottle!
Wow! You're on FIRE today, Lola!
10
HA
HA
HA
HA
HA
HA
Hmm . . .
They seem pretty intense.
TACO DON PEPE

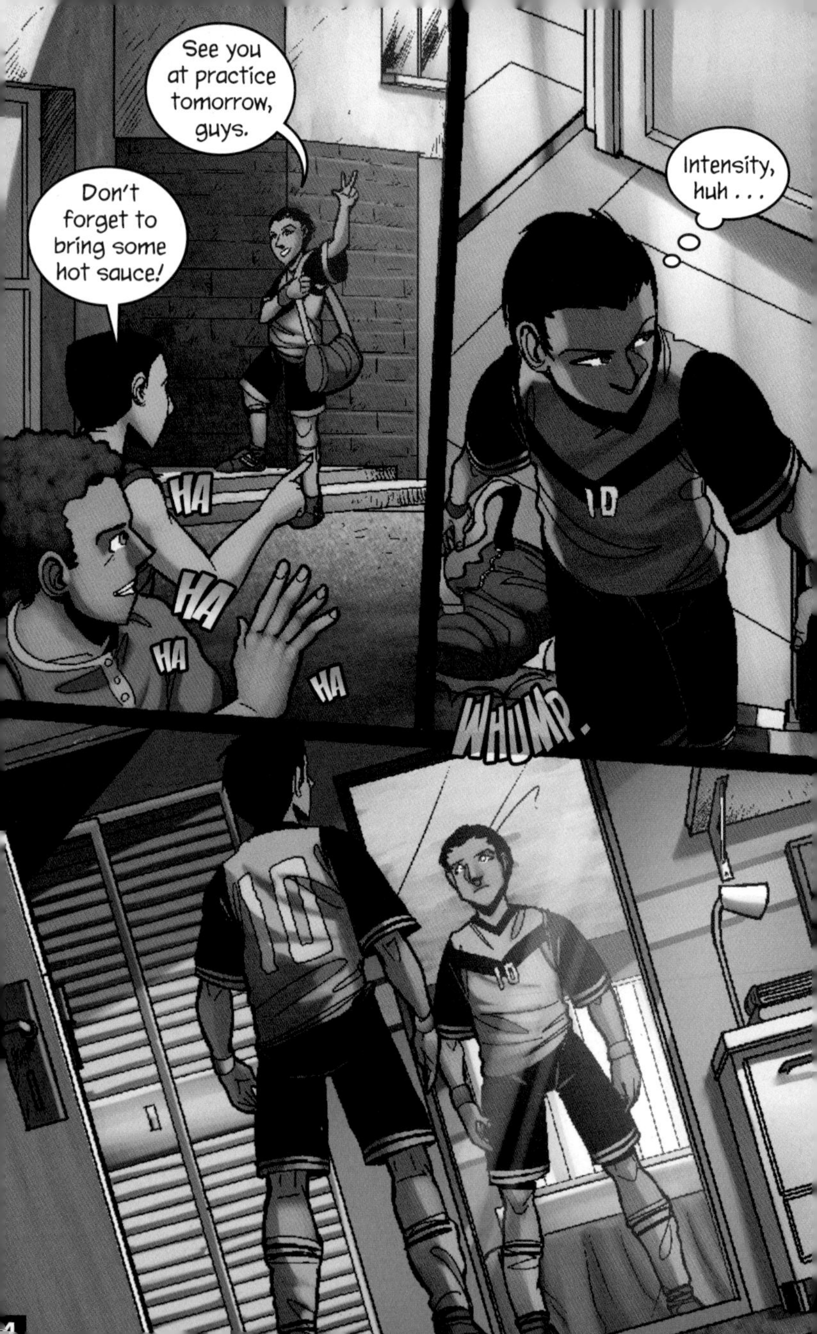
See you at practice tomorrow, guys.
Don't forget to bring some hot sauce!
HA
HA
HA
HA
Intensity, huh . . .
WHUMP.

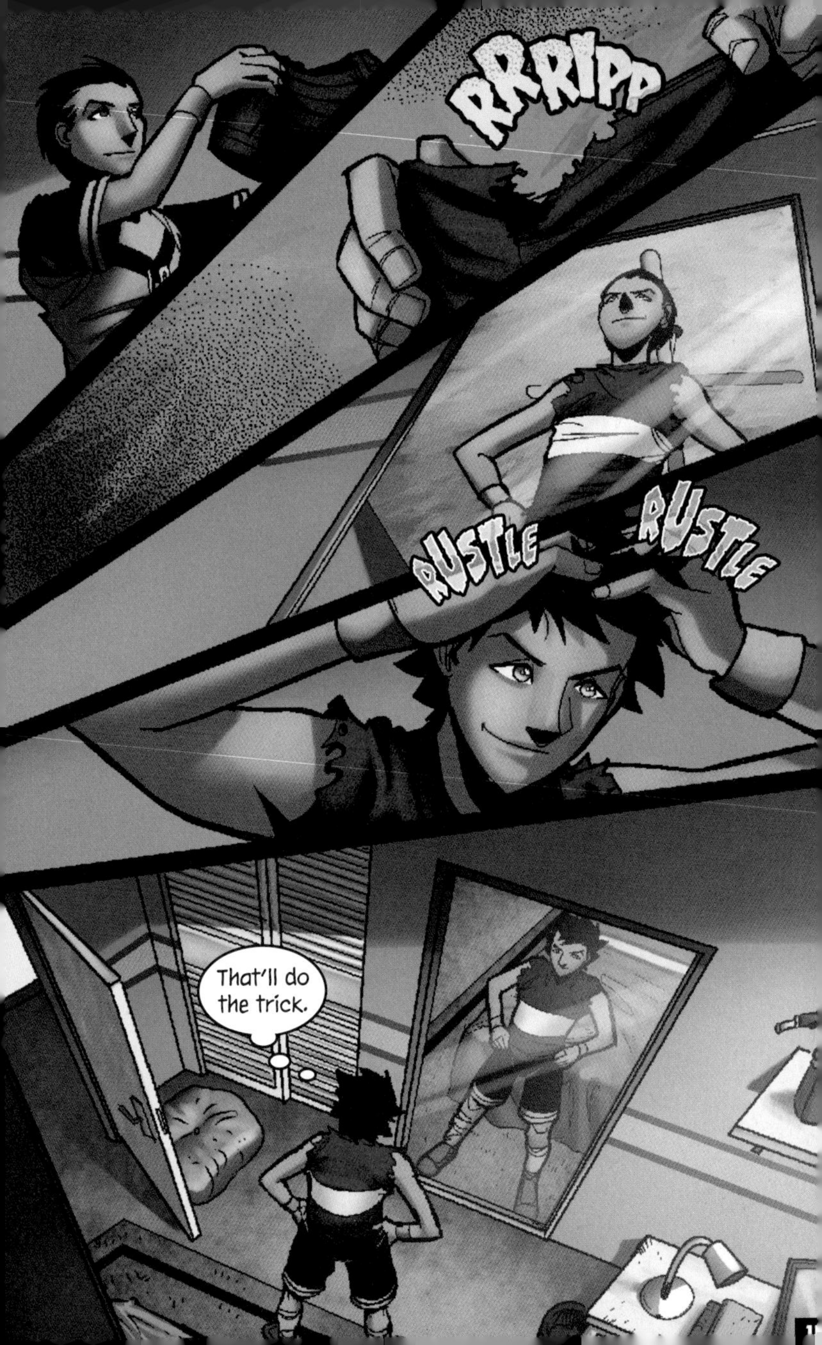
RRRIPP
RUSTLE
RUSTLE
That'll do the trick.

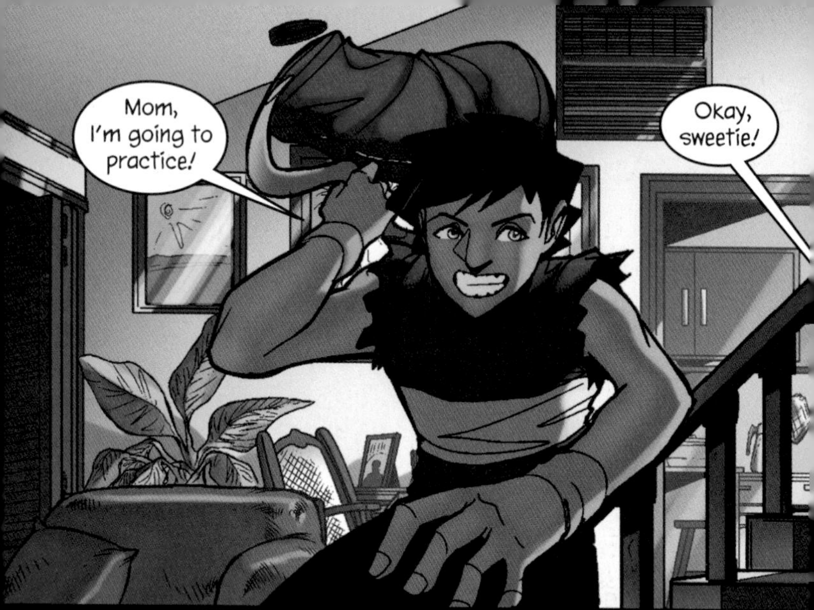
Mom, I'm going to practice!
Okay, sweetie!
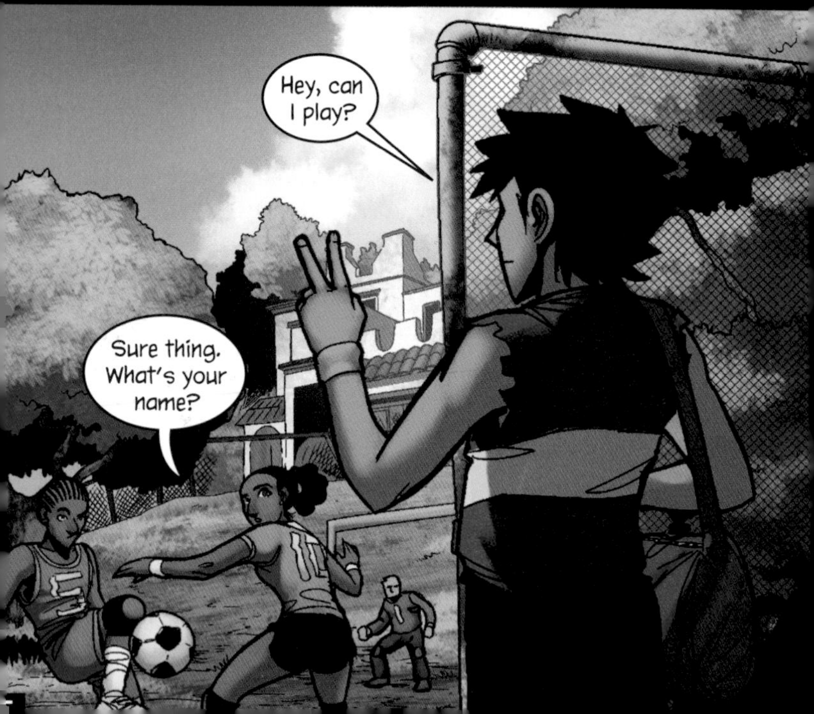
Hey, can I play?
Sure thing. What's your name?

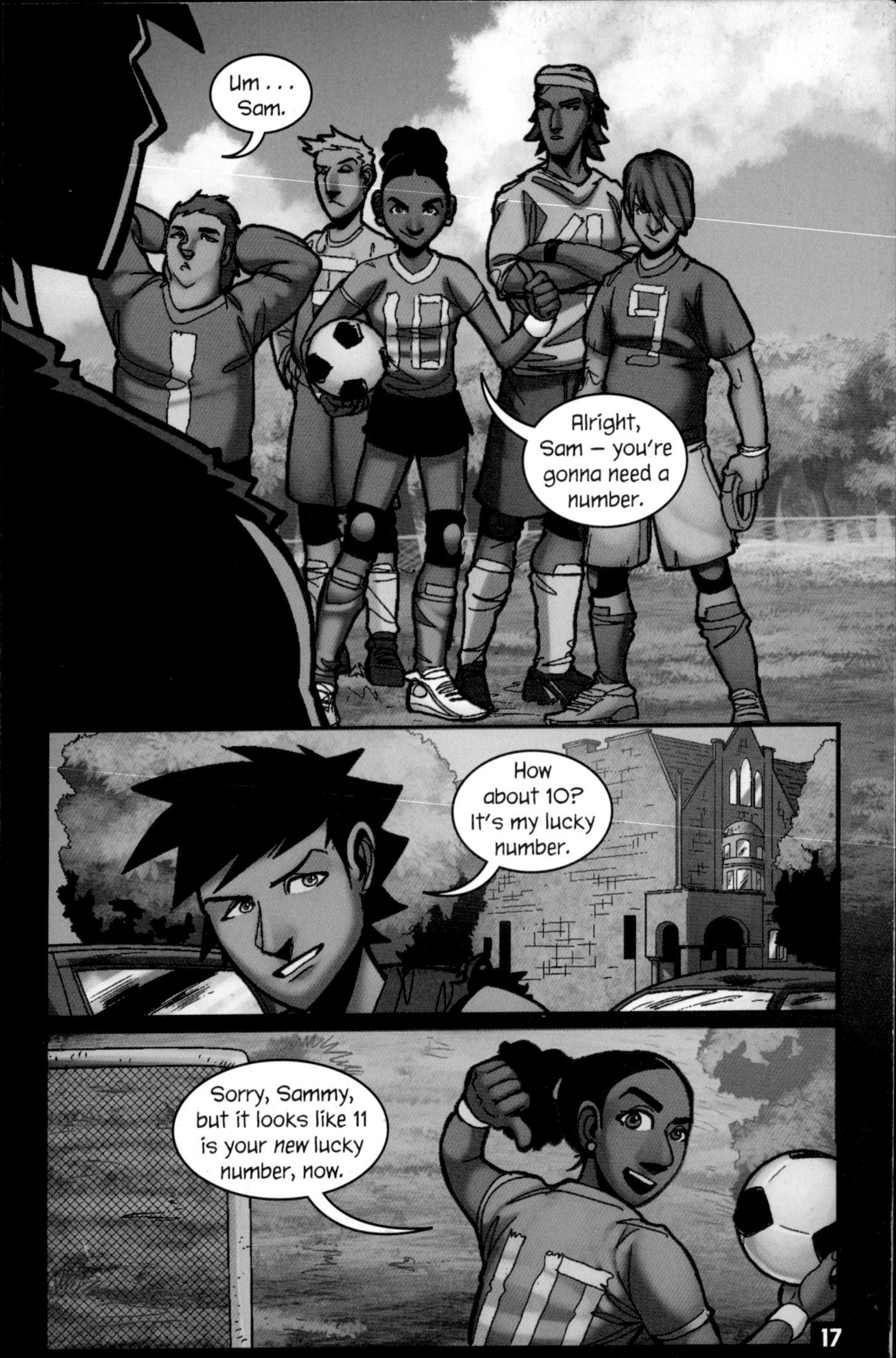
Um . . . Sam.
Alright, Sam — you're gonna need a number.
How about 10? It's my lucky number.
Sorry, Sammy, but it looks like 11 is your *new* lucky number, now.

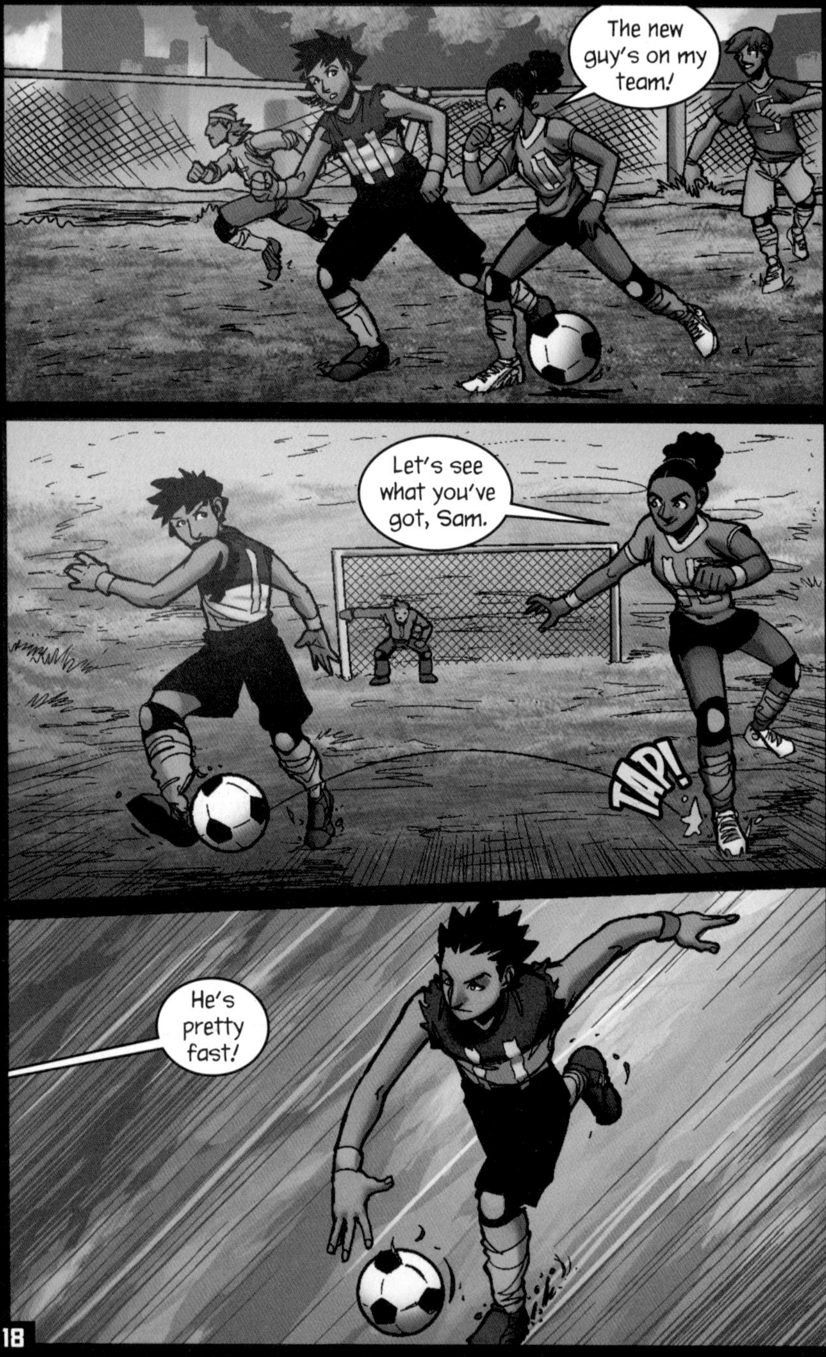
The new guy's on my team!
Let's see what you've got, Sam.
TAP!
He's pretty fast!

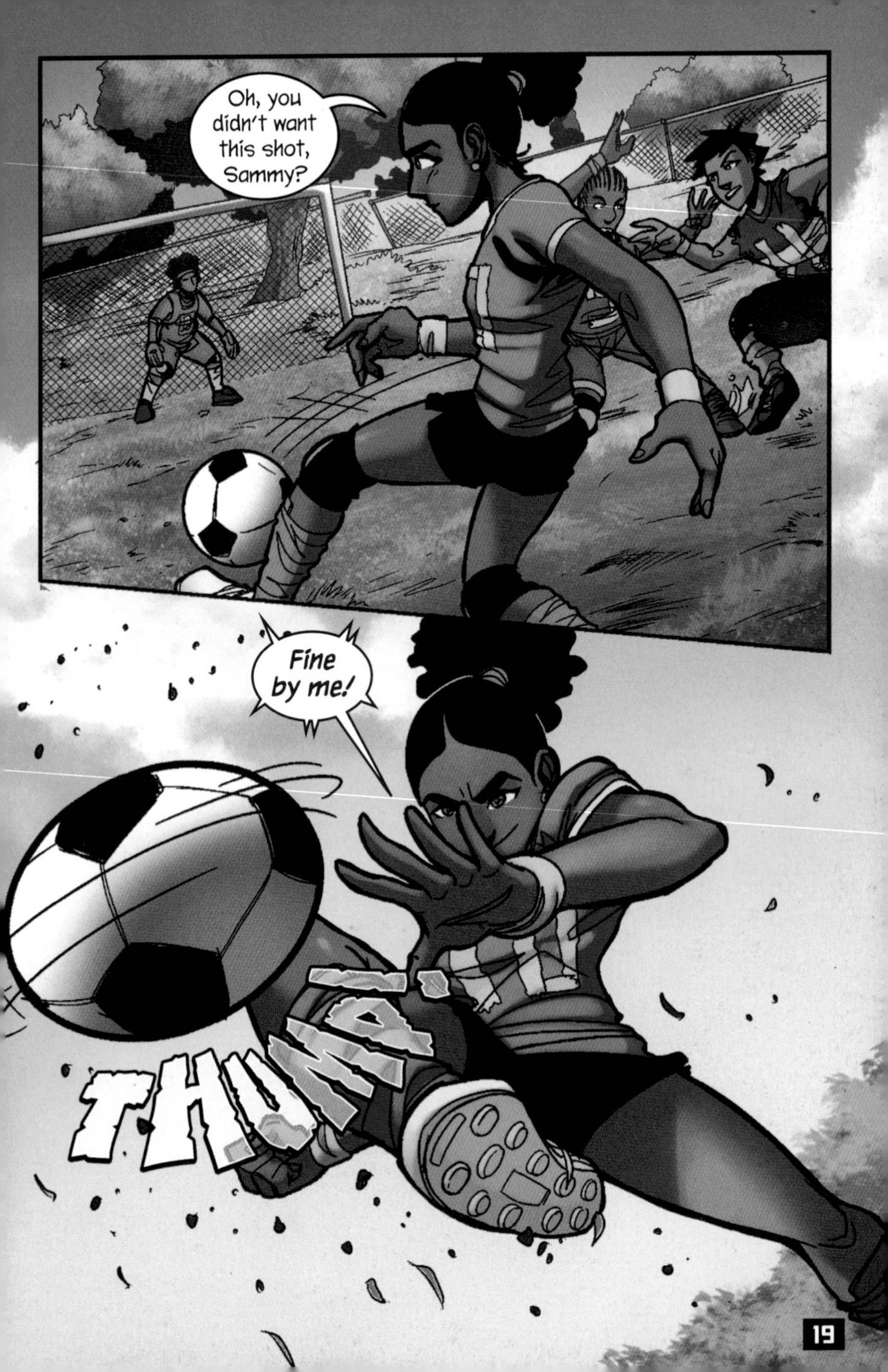
Oh, you didn't want this shot, Sammy?
Fine by me!
THUMP!

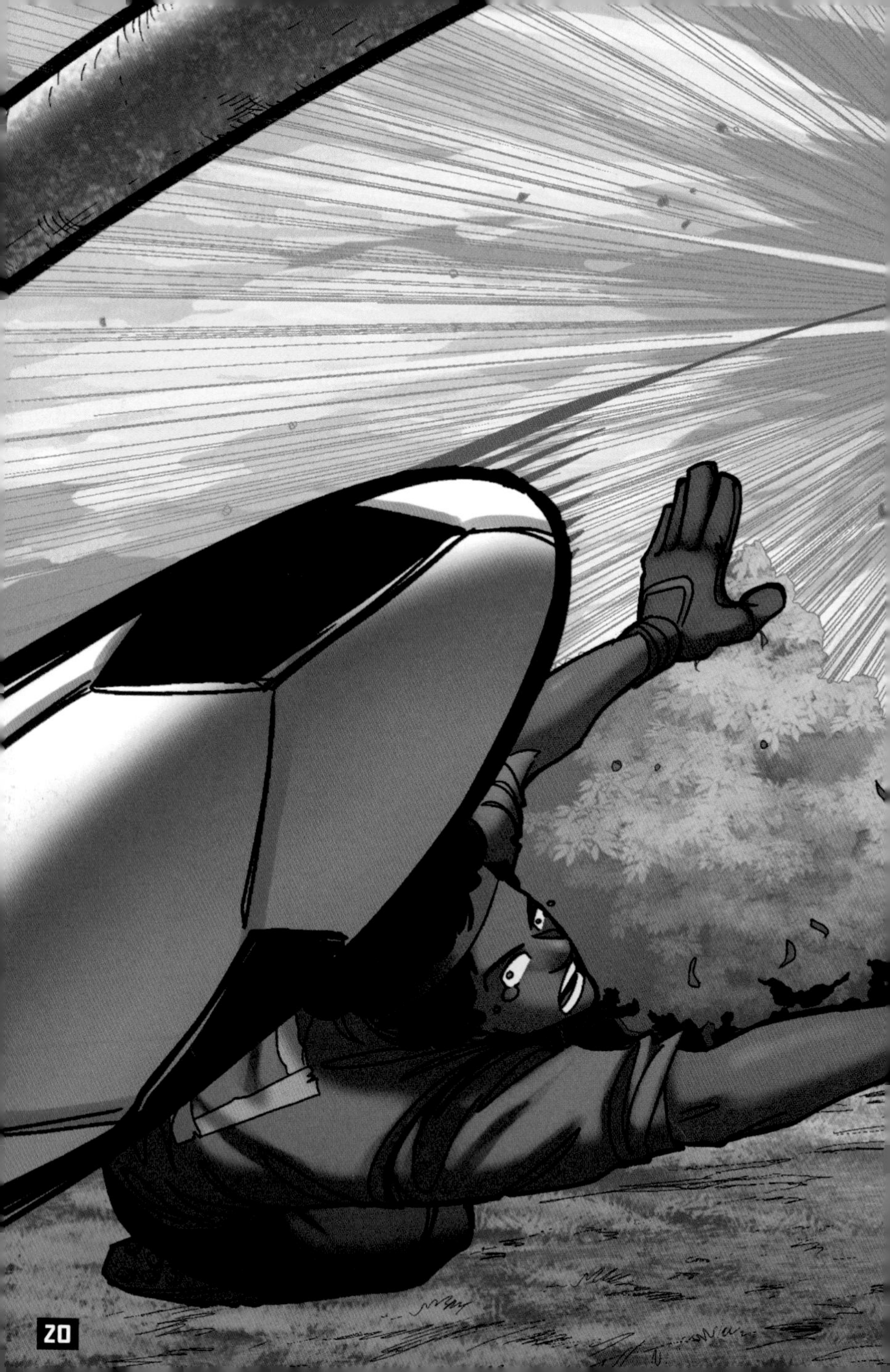

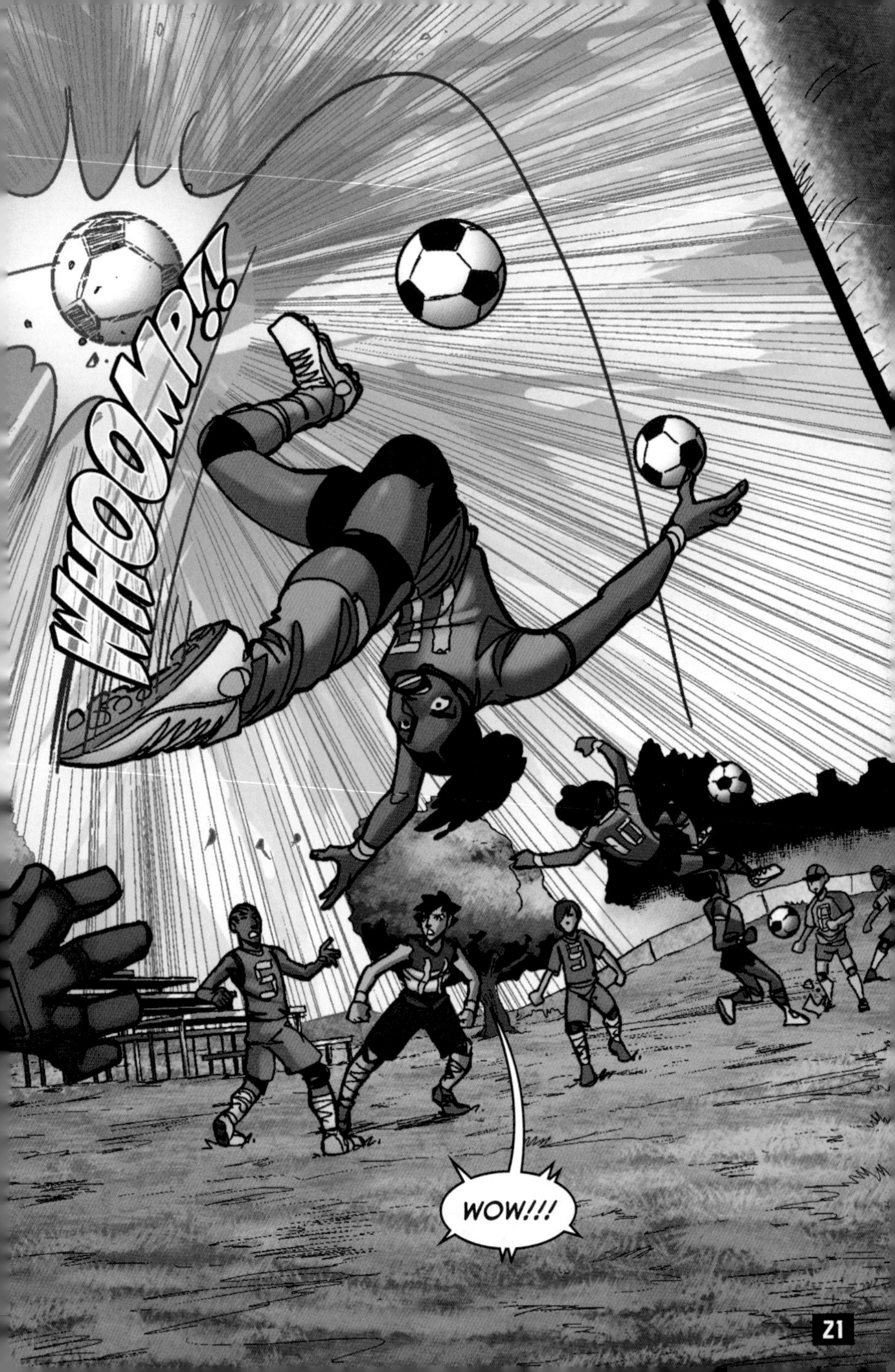
WHOOMP!!
WOW!!!

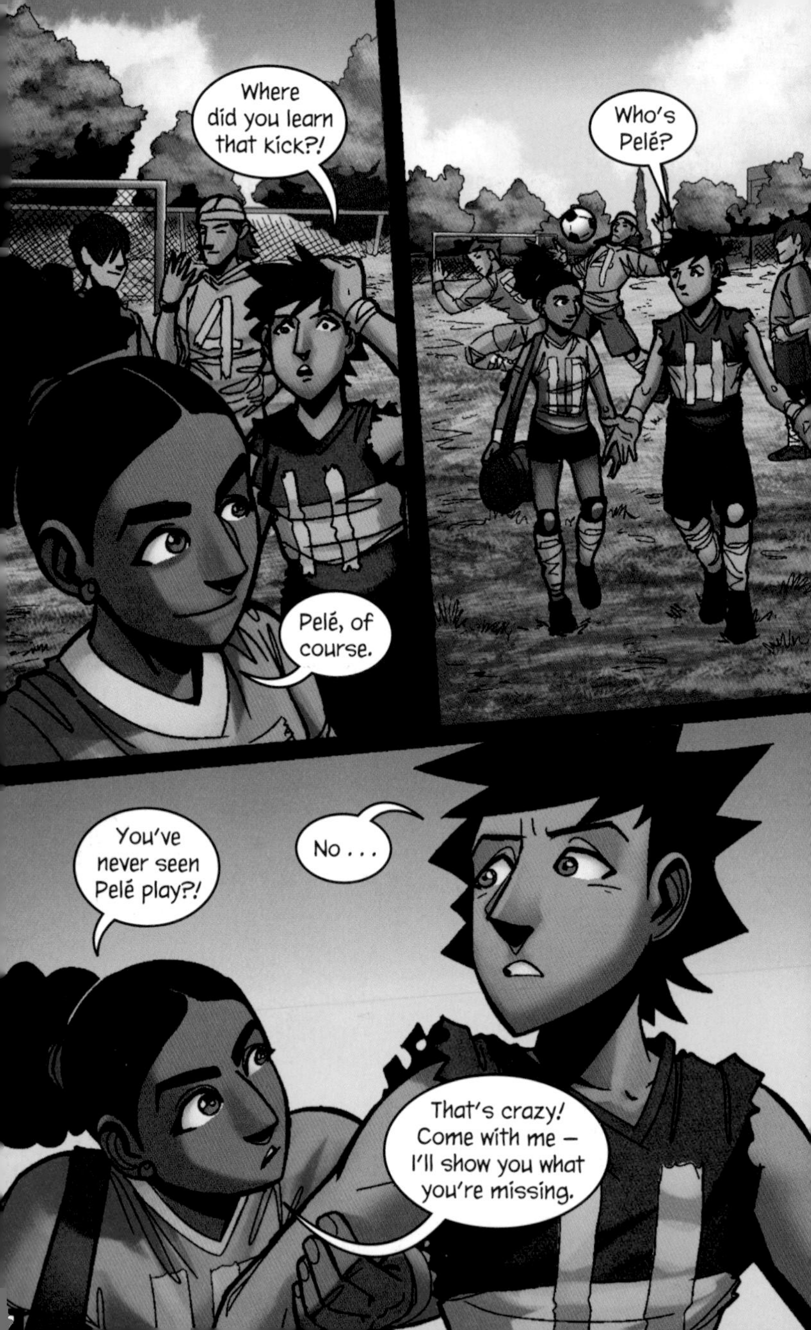
Where did you learn that kick?!
Pelé, of course.
Who's Pelé?
You've never seen Pelé play?!
No . . .
That's crazy! Come with me — I'll show you what you're missing.

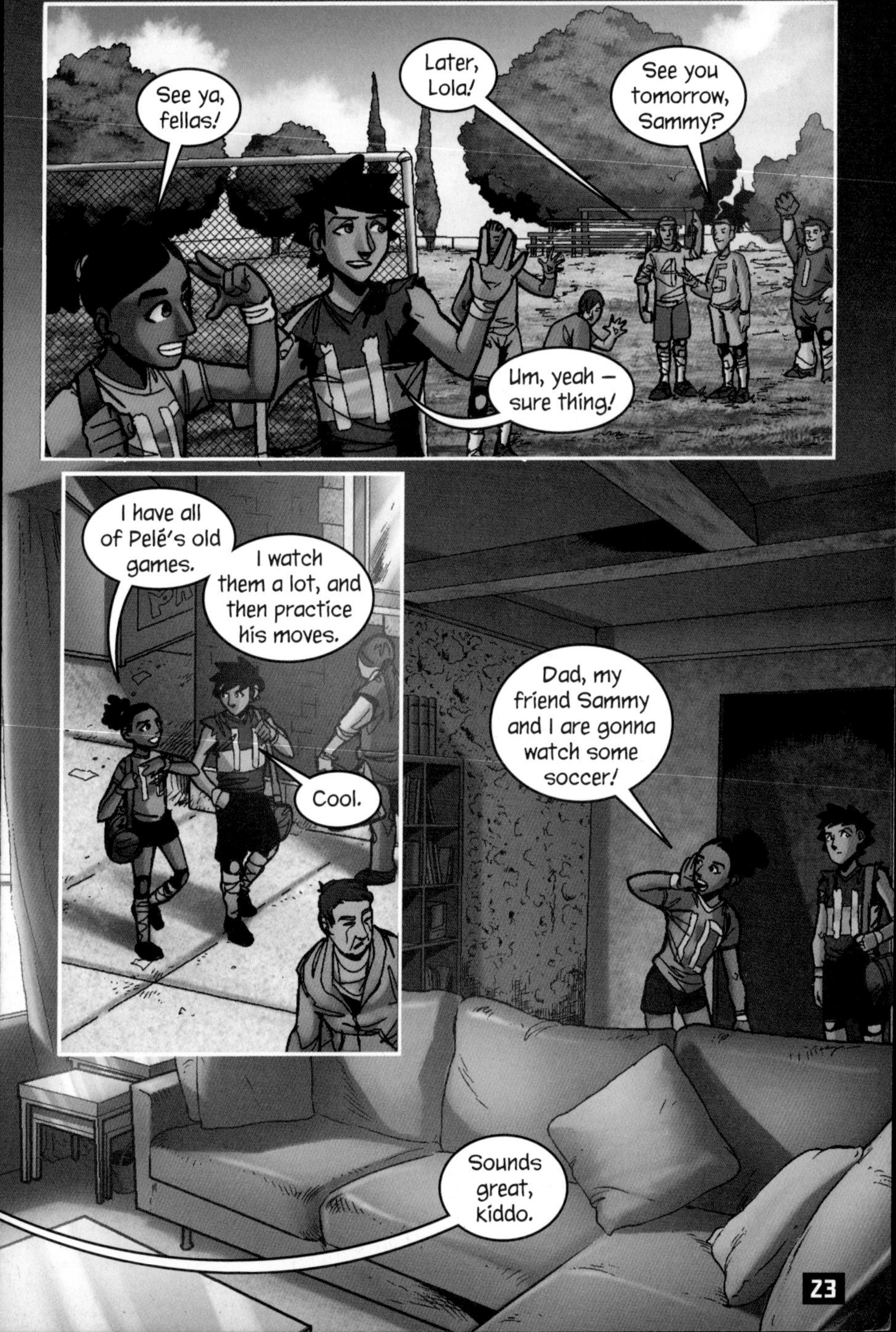

See ya, fellas!
Later, Lola!
See you tomorrow, Sammy?
Um, yeah — sure thing!
I have all of Pelé's old games.
I watch them a lot, and then practice his moves.
Cool.
Dad, my friend Sammy and I are gonna watch some soccer!
Sounds great, kiddo.

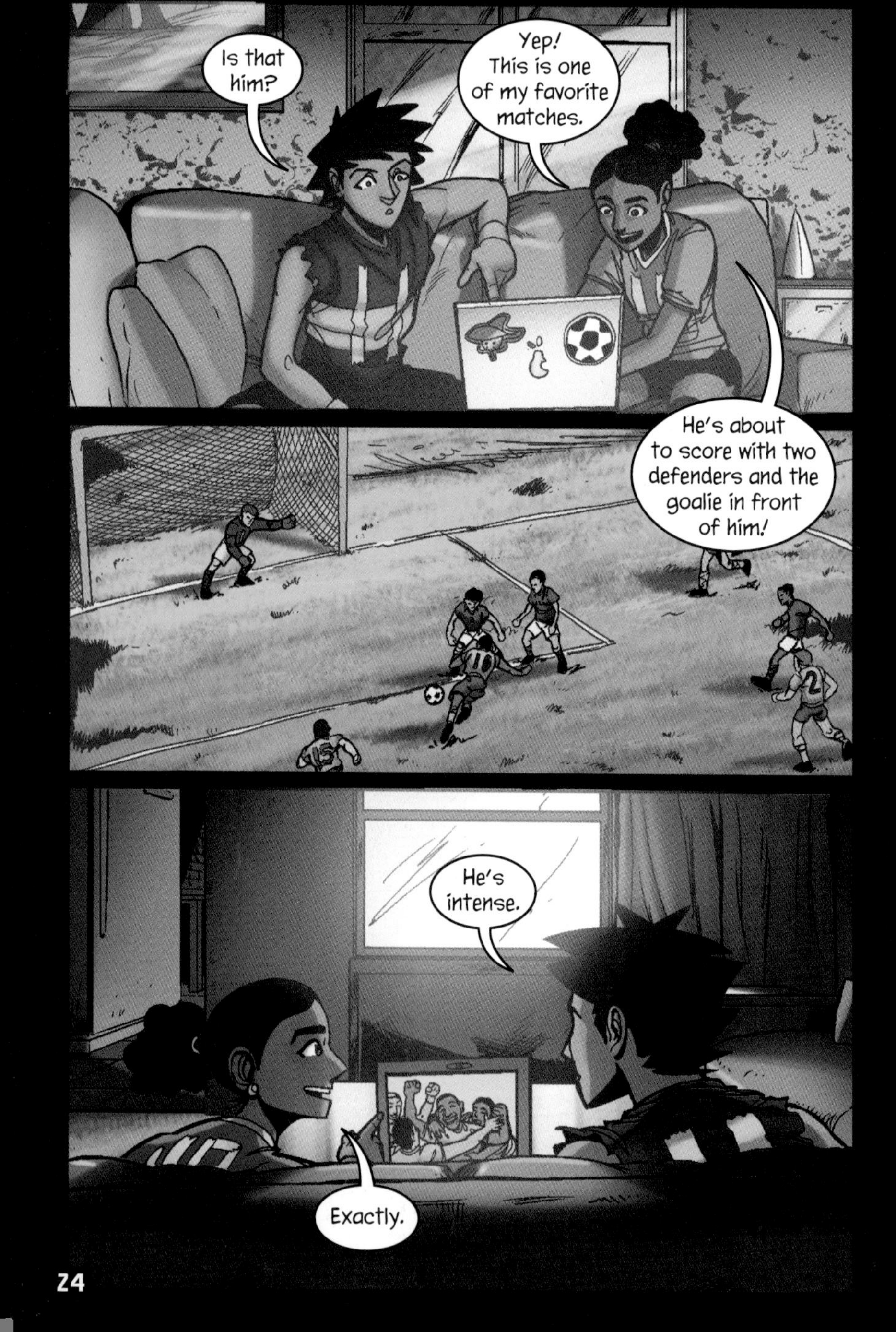
Is that him?
Yep! This is one of my favorite matches.
He's about to score with two defenders and the goalie in front of him!
He's intense.
Exactly.

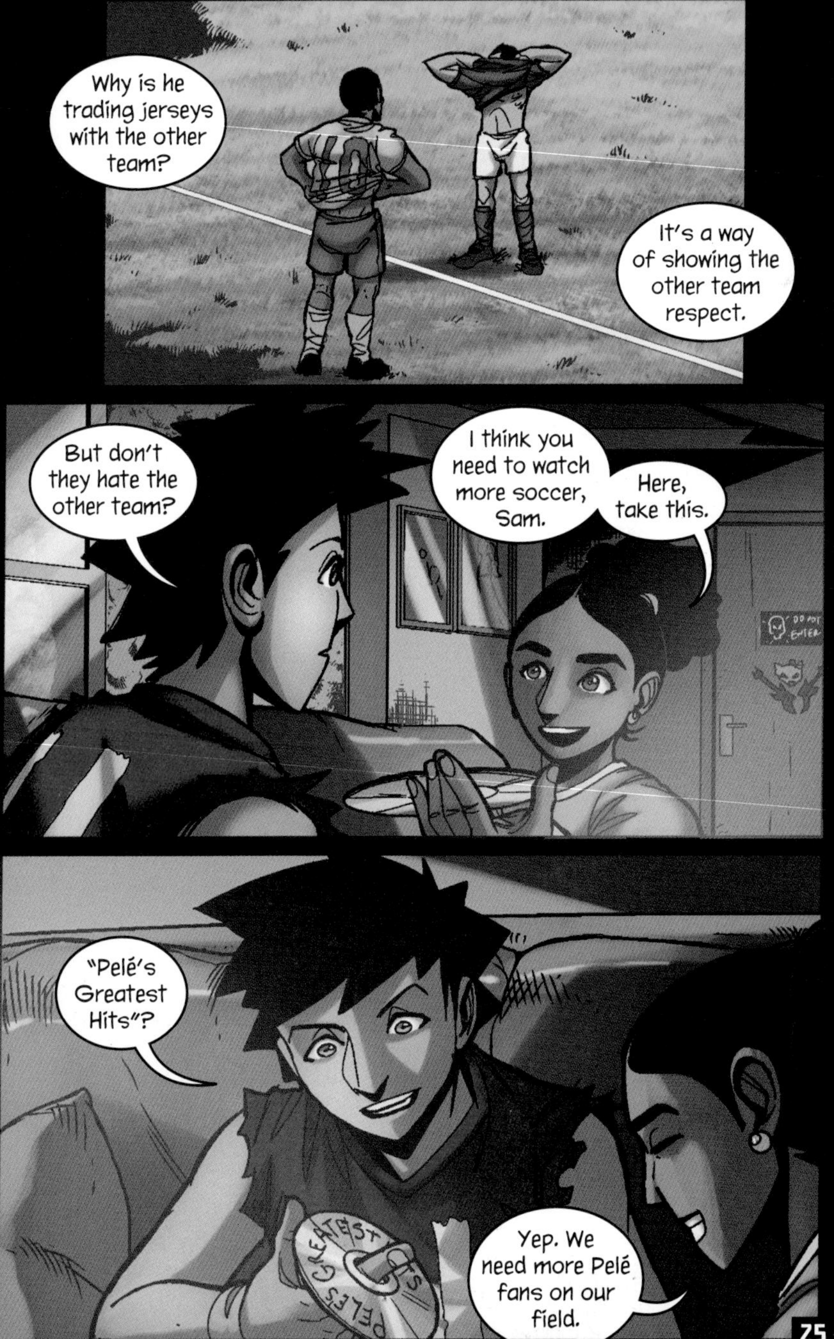
Why is he trading jerseys with the other team?
It's a way of showing the other team respect.
But don't they hate the other team?
I think you need to watch more soccer, Sam.
Here, take this.
"Pelé's Greatest Hits"?
Yep. We need more Pelé fans on our field.

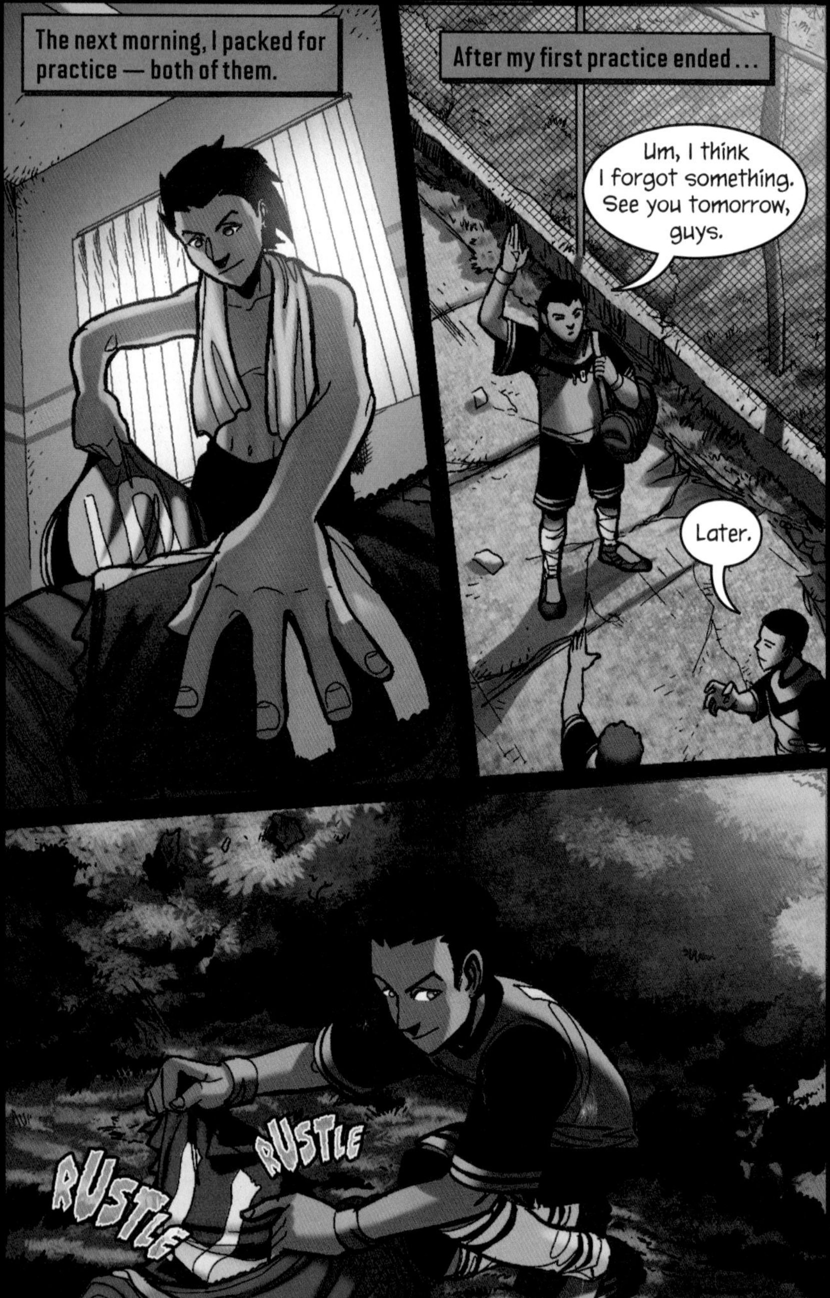

The next morning, I packed for practice — both of them.
After my first practice ended . . .
Um, I think I forgot something. See you tomorrow, guys.
Later.
RUSTLE
RUSTLE
RUSTLE

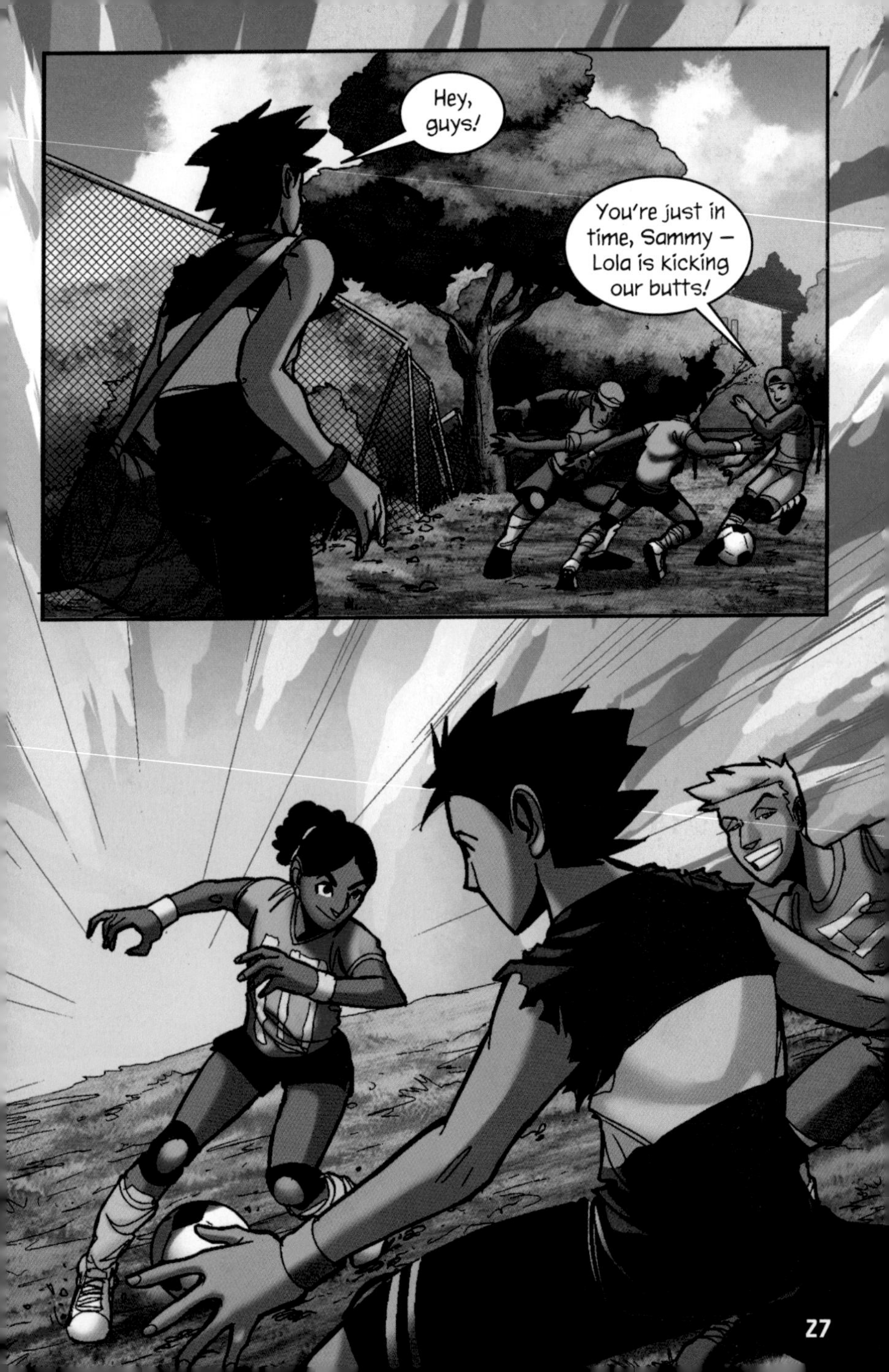
Hey, guys!
You're just in time, Sammy — Lola is kicking our butts!

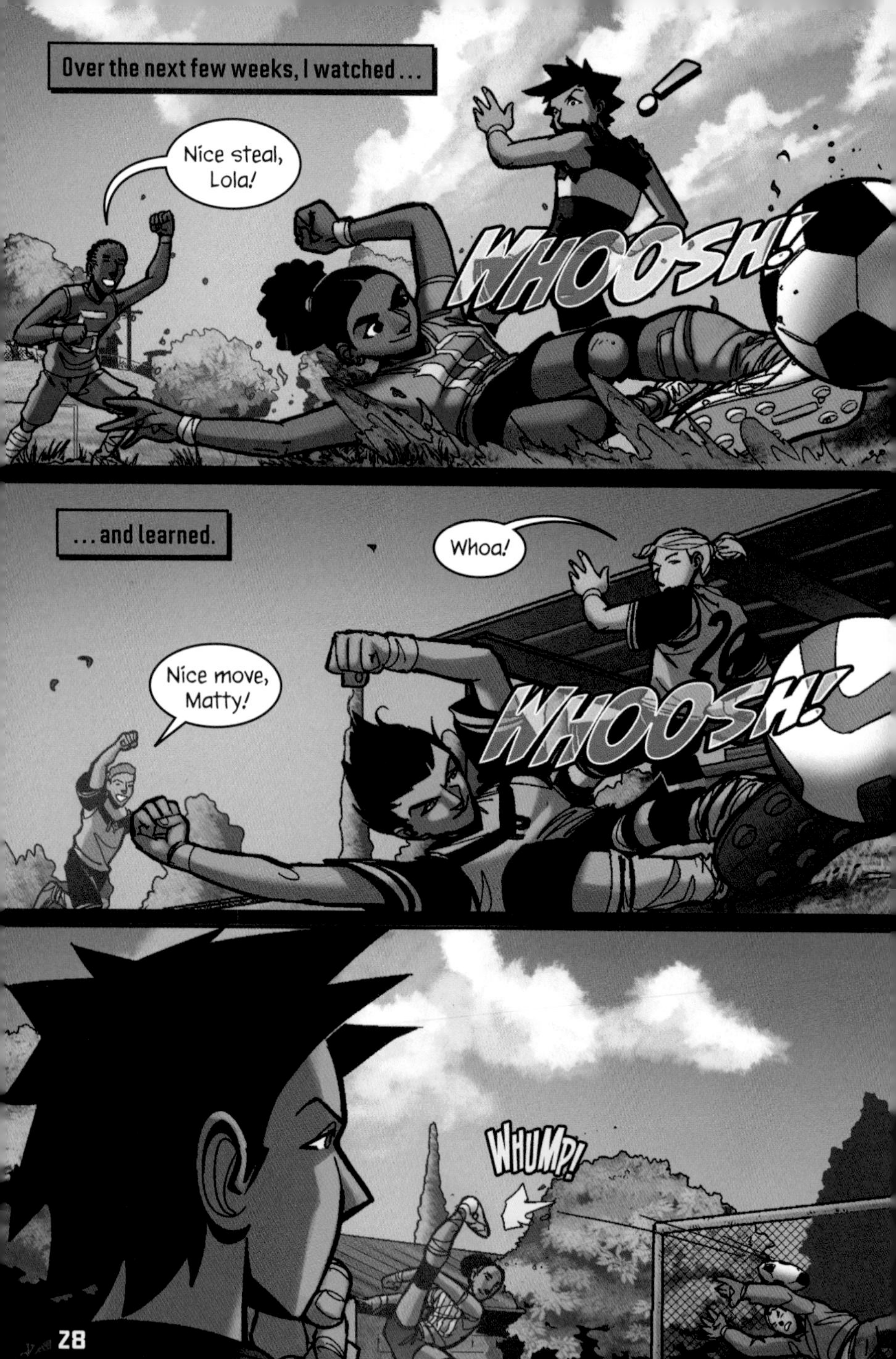
Over the next few weeks, I watched . . .
Nice steal, Lola!
WHOOSH!
. . . and learned.
Whoa!
Nice move, Matty!
WHOOSH!
WHUMP!

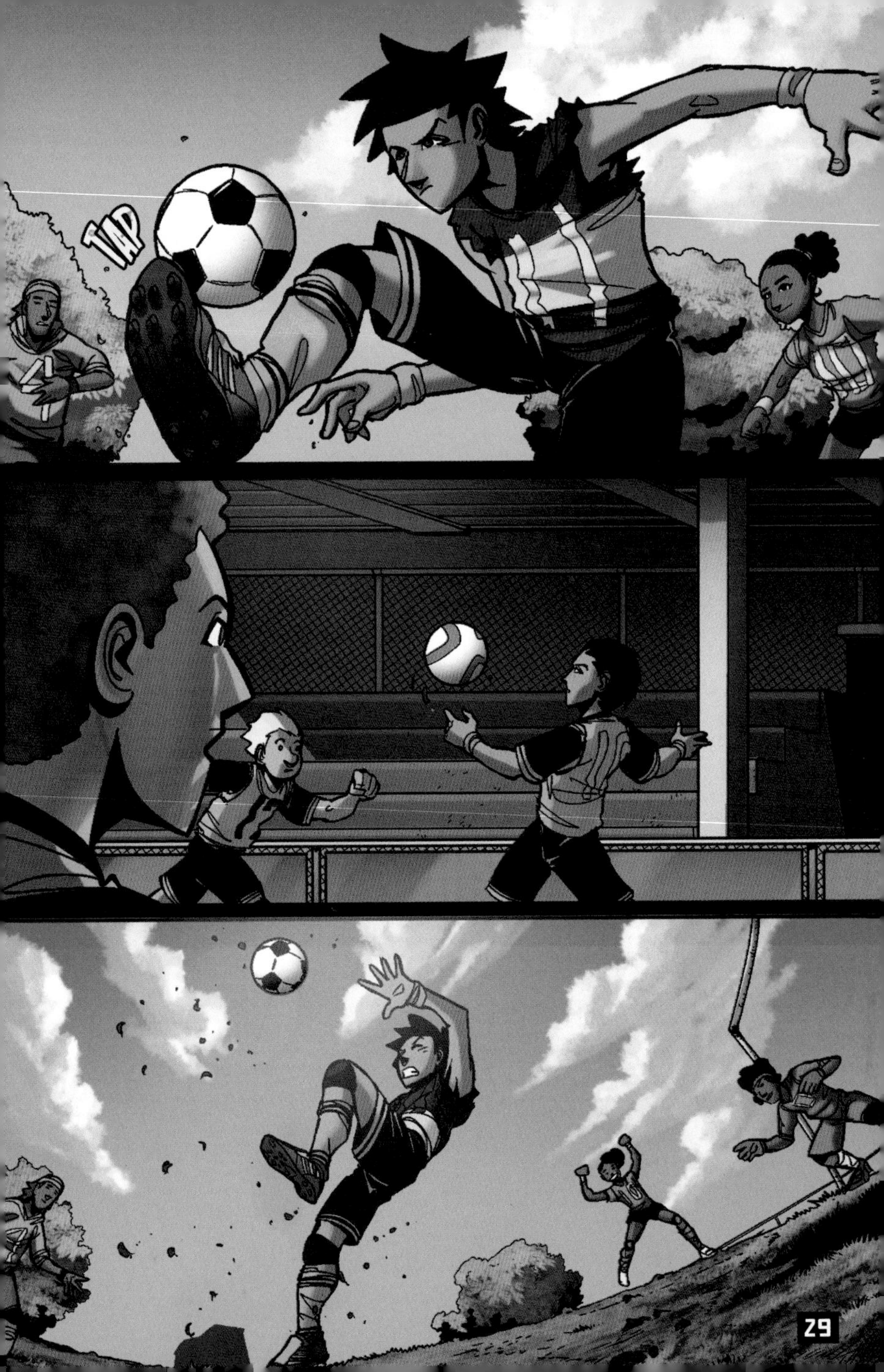
TAP

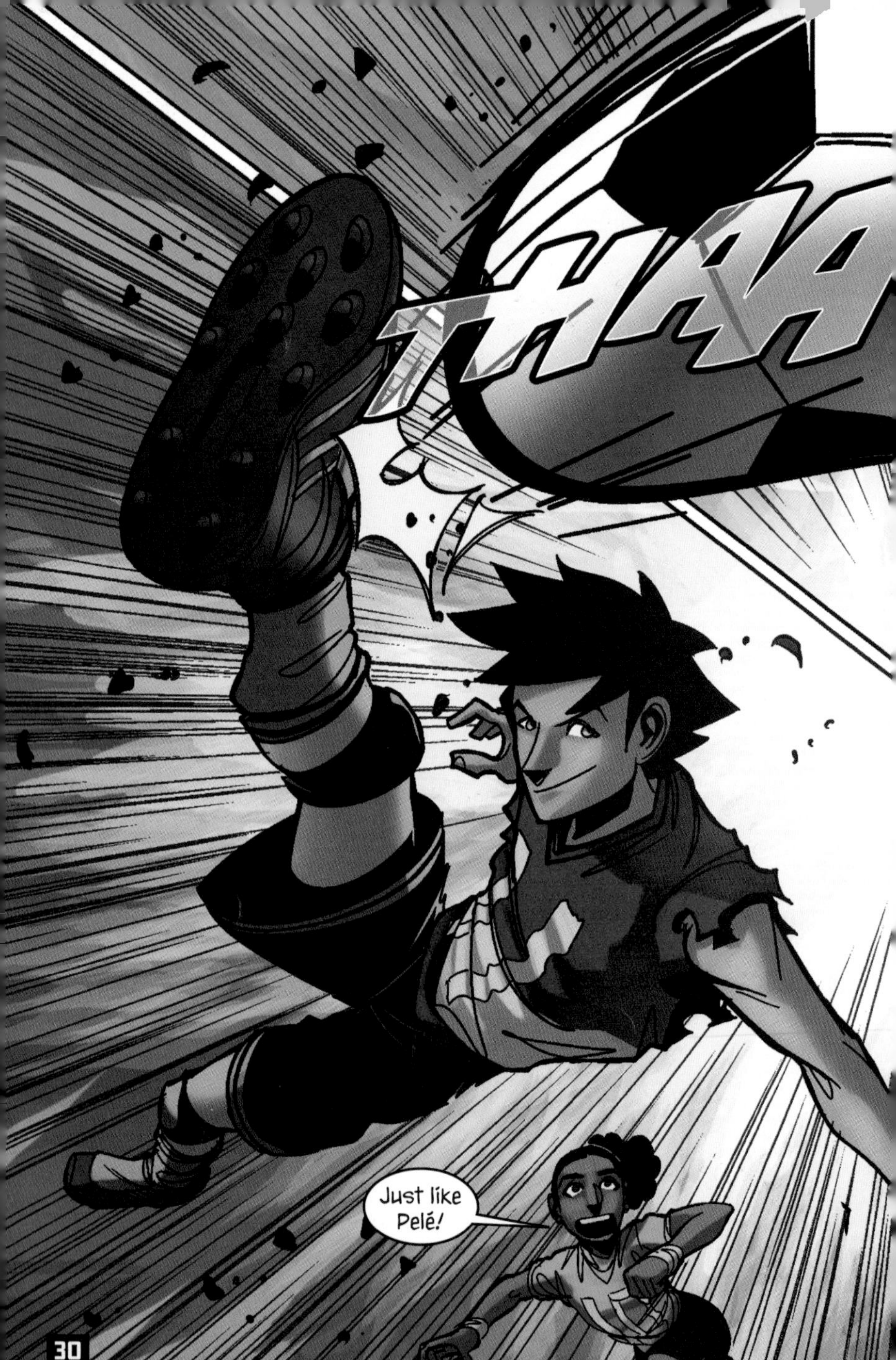
THAA
Just like Pelé!

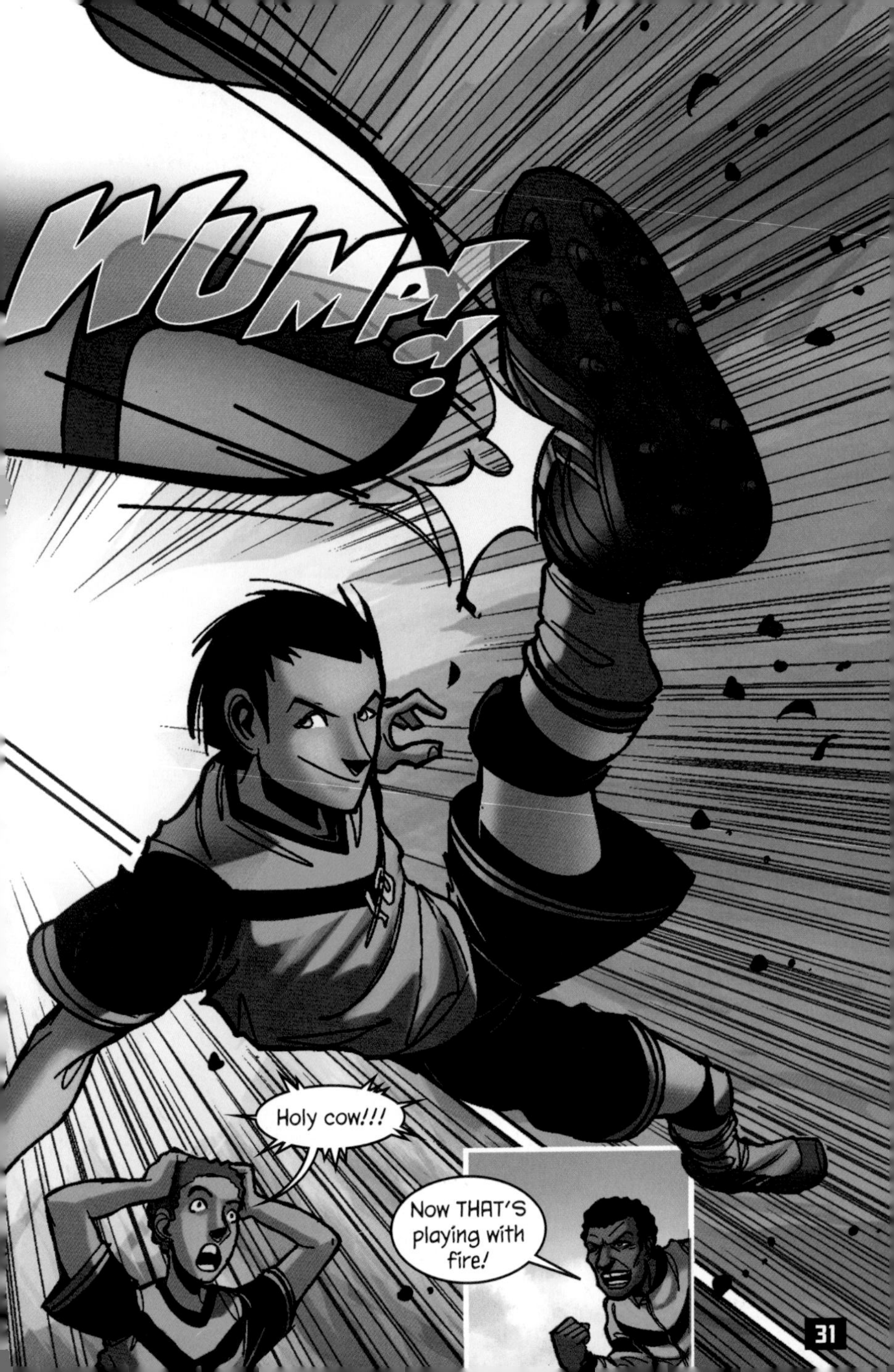
WUMP!
Holy cow!!!
Now THAT'S playing with fire!

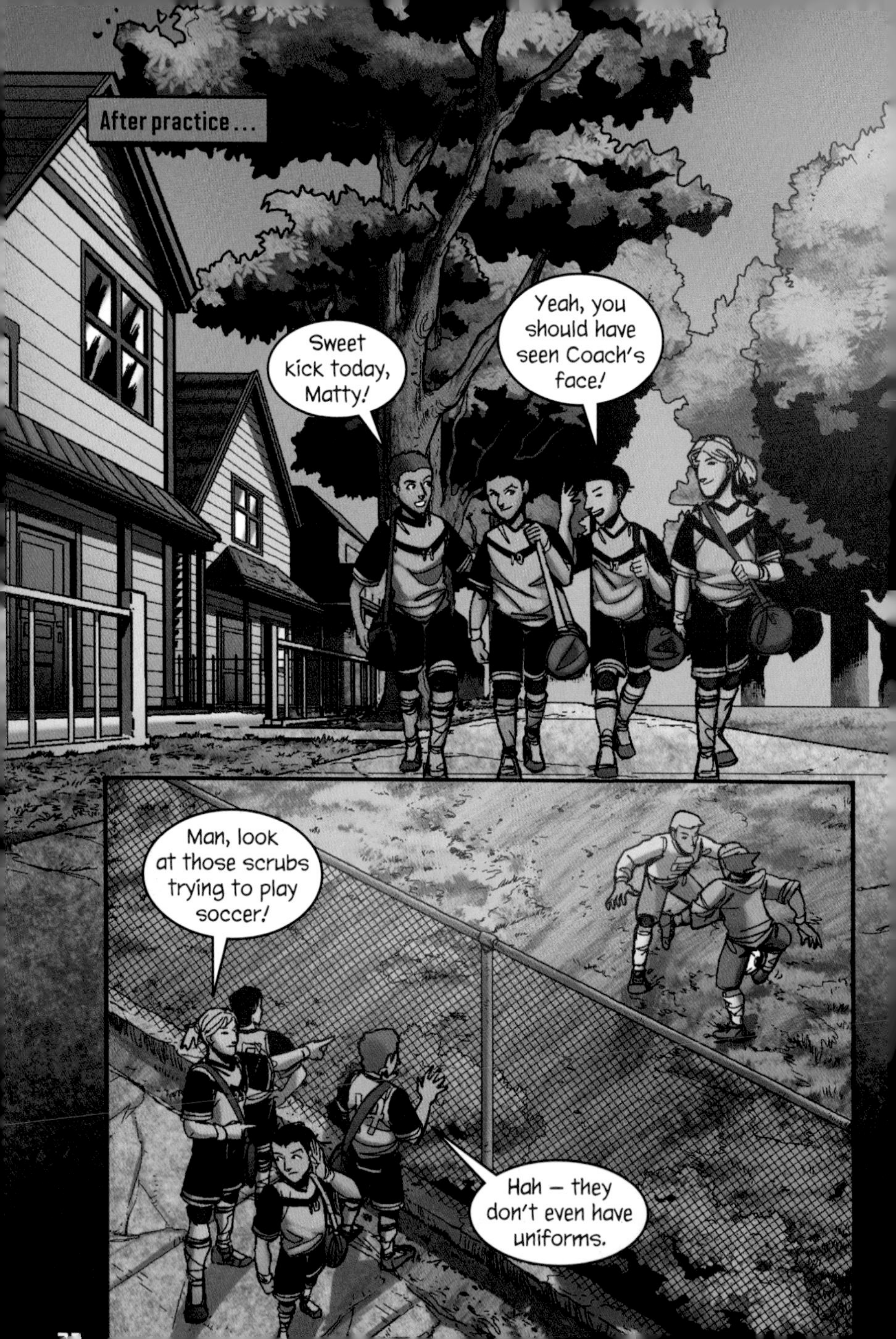
After practice . . .
Sweet kick today, Matty!
Yeah, you should have seen Coach's face!
Man, look at those scrubs trying to play soccer!
Hah — they don't even have uniforms.

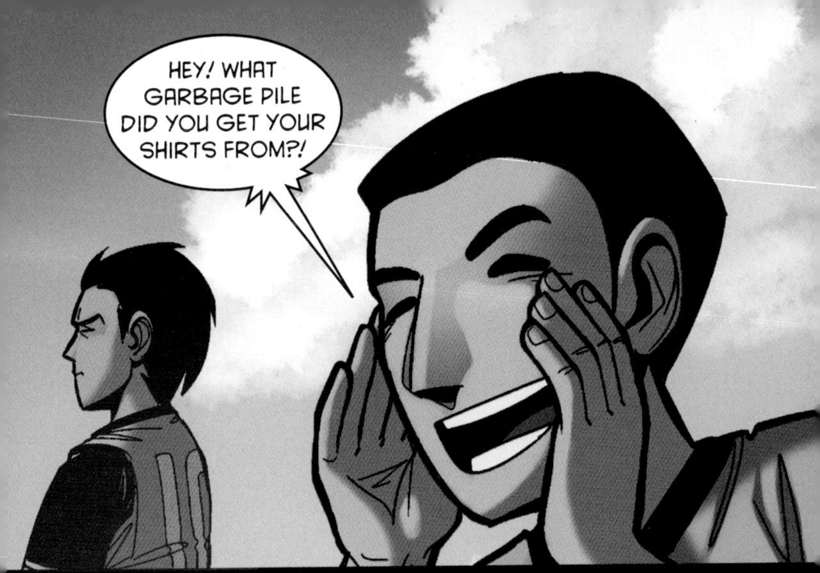
HEY! WHAT GARBAGE PILE DID YOU GET YOUR SHIRTS FROM?!

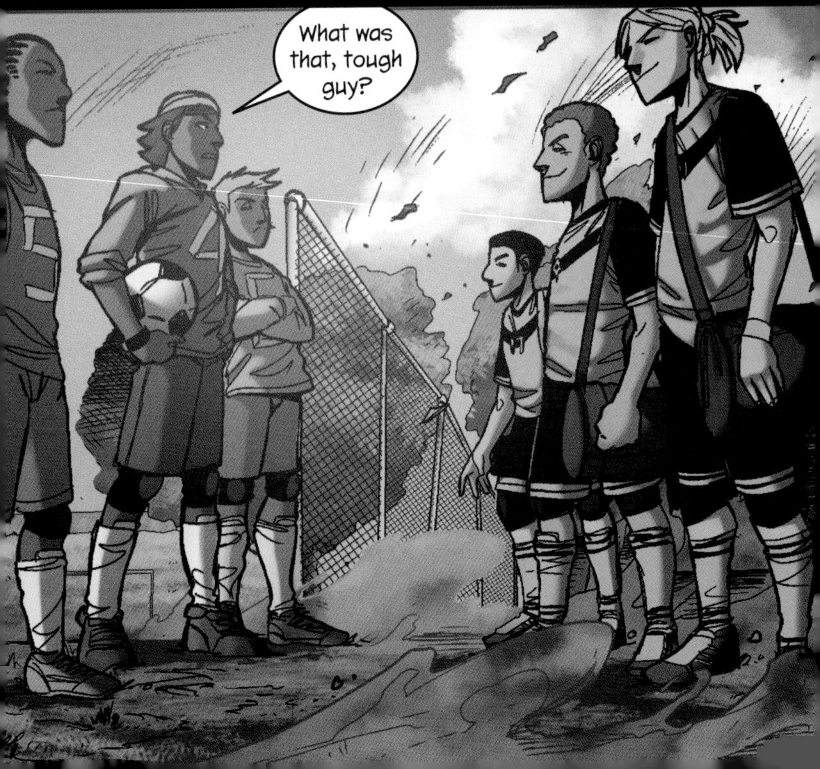
What was that, tough guy?

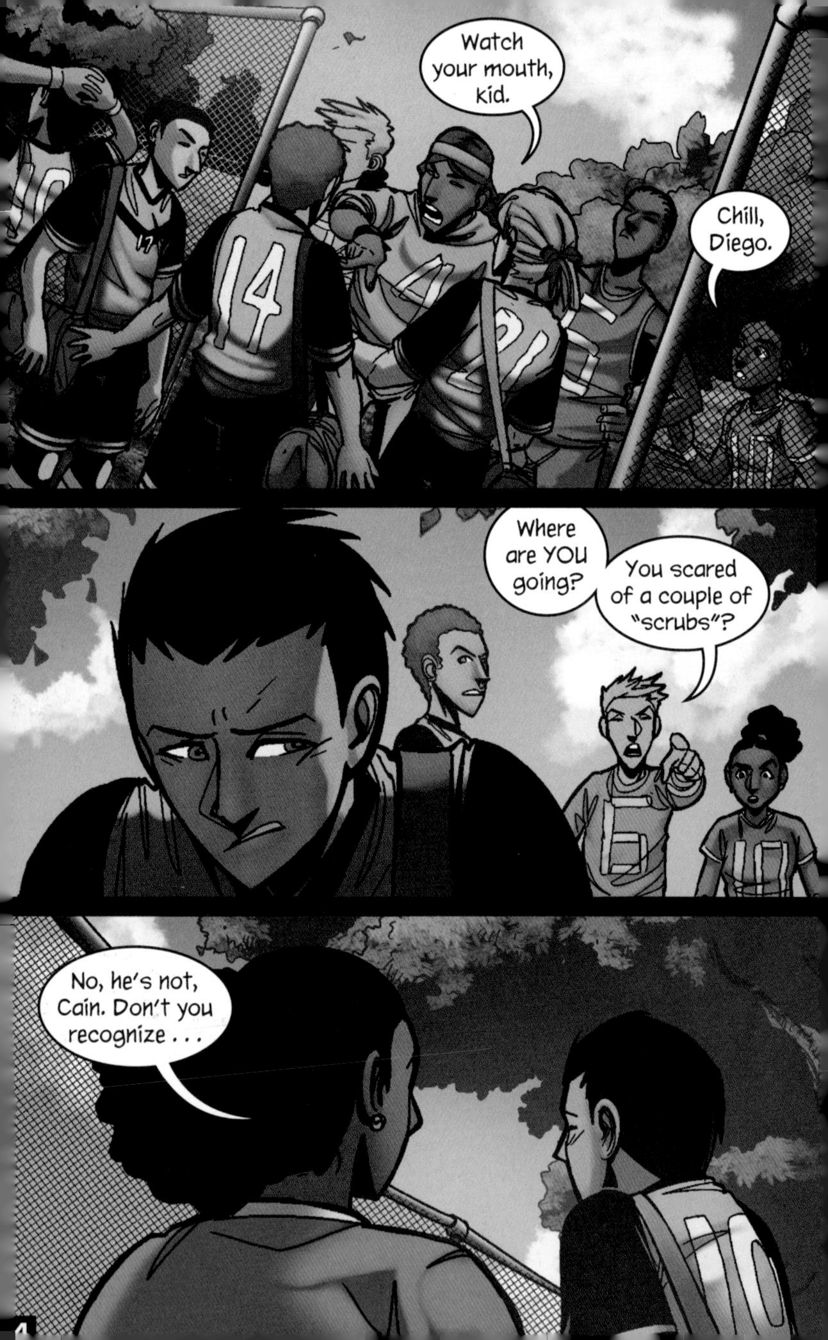
Watch your mouth, kid.
Chill, Diego.
Where are YOU going?
You scared of a couple of "scrubs"?
No, he's not, Cain. Don't you recognize . . .

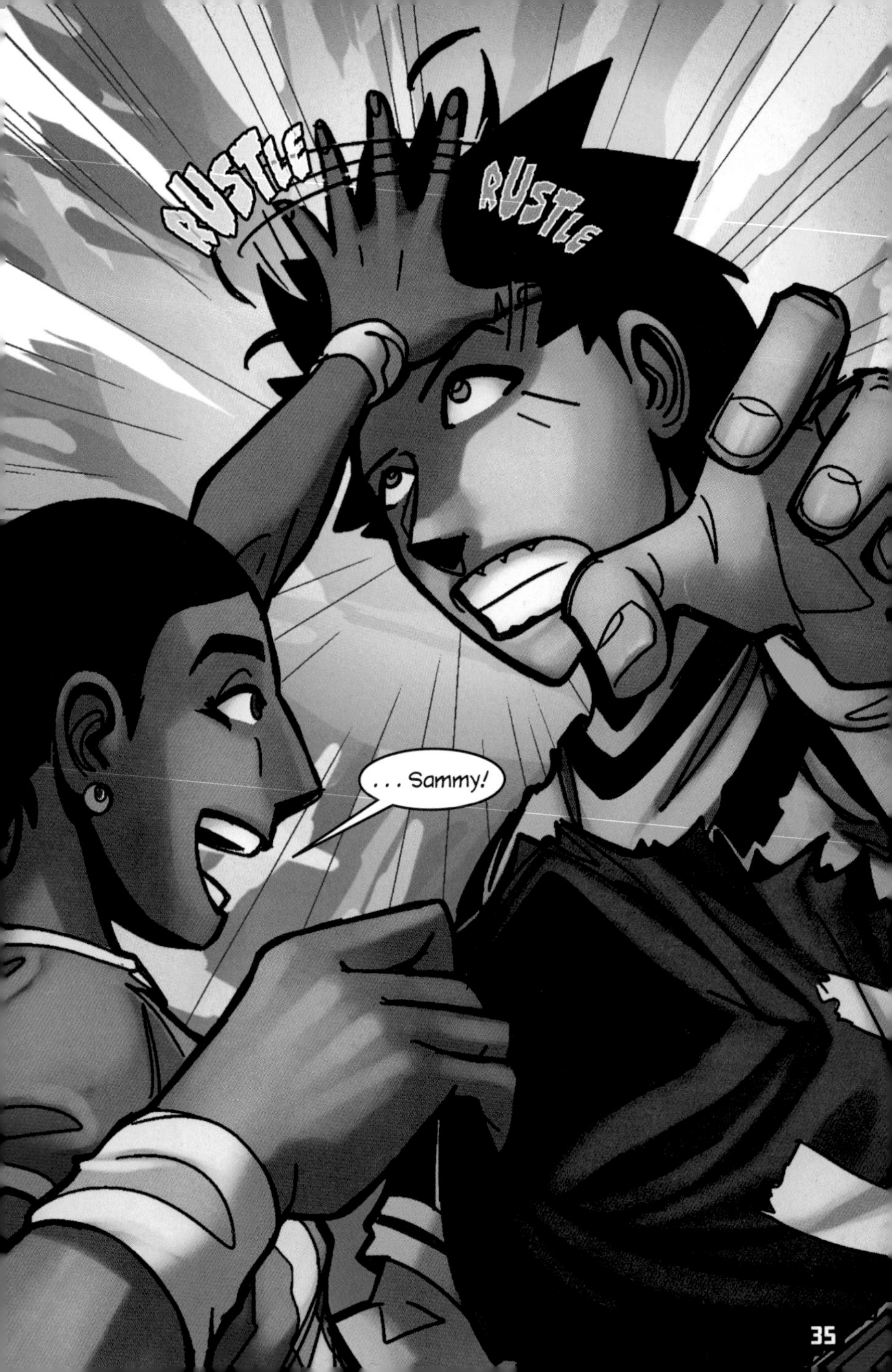
RUSTLE
RUSTLE
. . . Sammy!

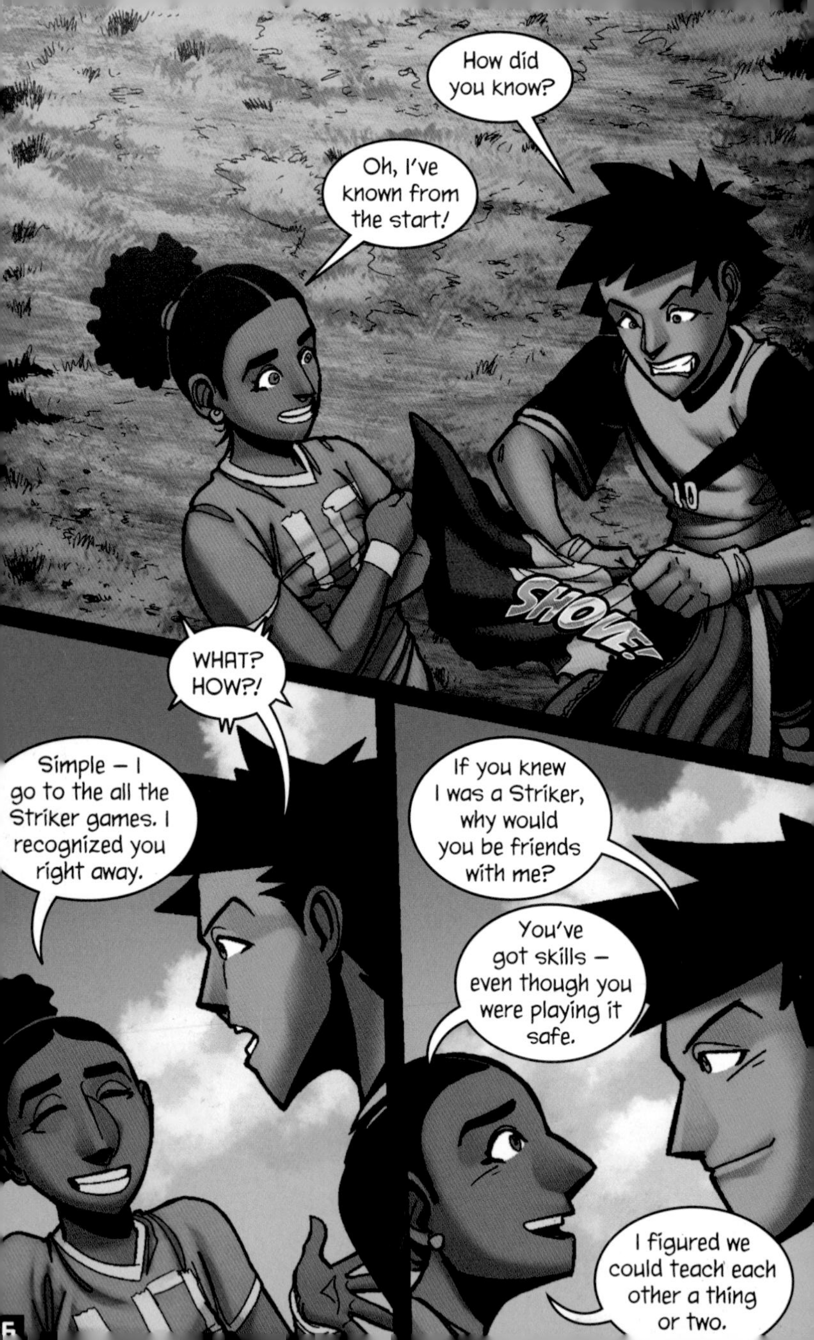
How did you know?
Oh, I've known from the start!
SHOVE!
WHAT? HOW?!
Simple — I go to the all the Striker games. I recognized you right away.
If you knew I was a Striker, why would you be friends with me?
You've got skills — even though you were playing it safe.
I figured we could teach each other a thing or two.

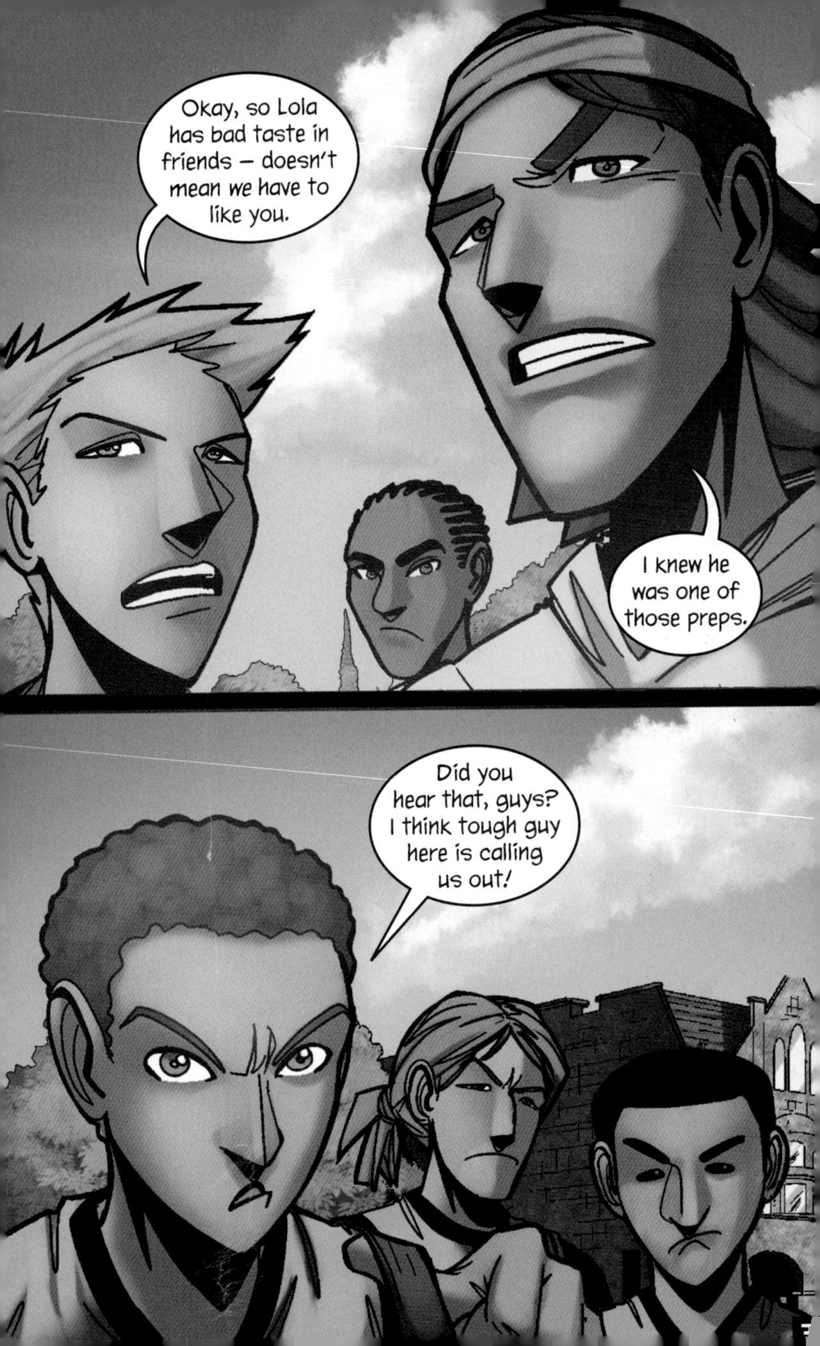
Okay, so Lola has bad taste in friends — doesn't mean we have to like you.
I knew he was one of those preps.
Did you hear that, guys? I think tough guy here is calling us out!

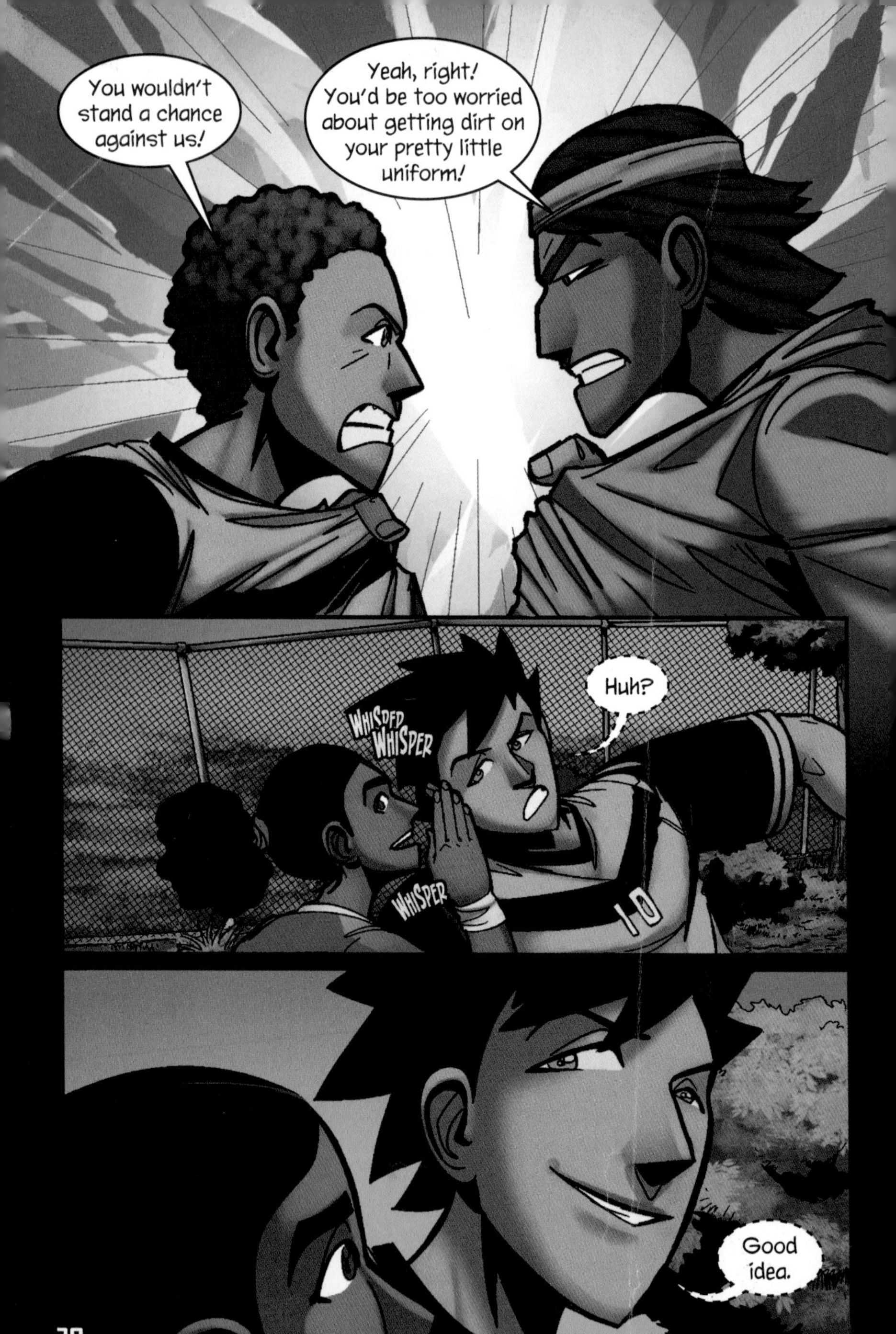
You wouldn't stand a chance against us!
Yeah, right! You'd be too worried about getting dirt on your pretty little uniform!
WHISPER
WHISPER
Huh?
Good idea.

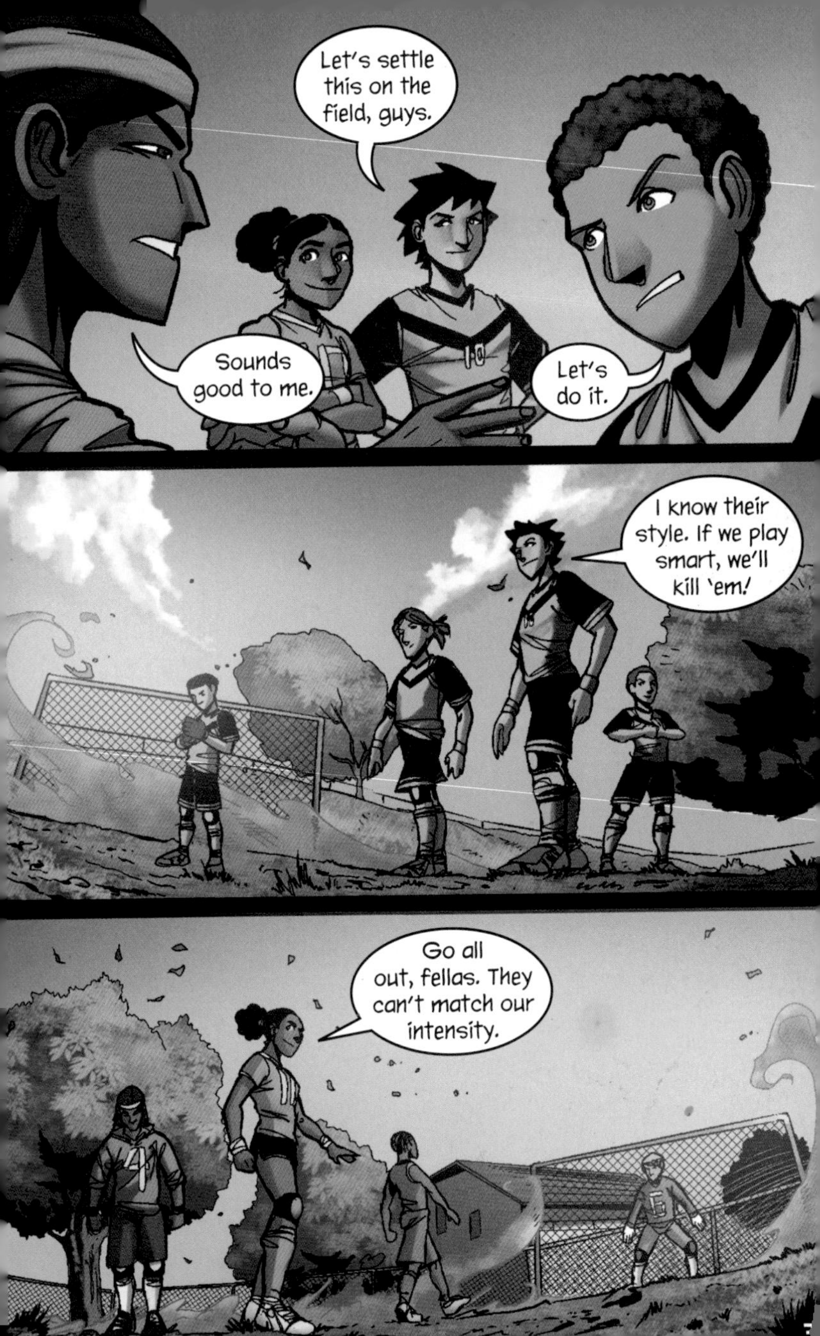

Let's settle this on the field, guys.
Sounds good to me.
Let's do it.
I know their style. If we play smart, we'll kill 'em!
Go all out, fellas. They can't match our intensity.

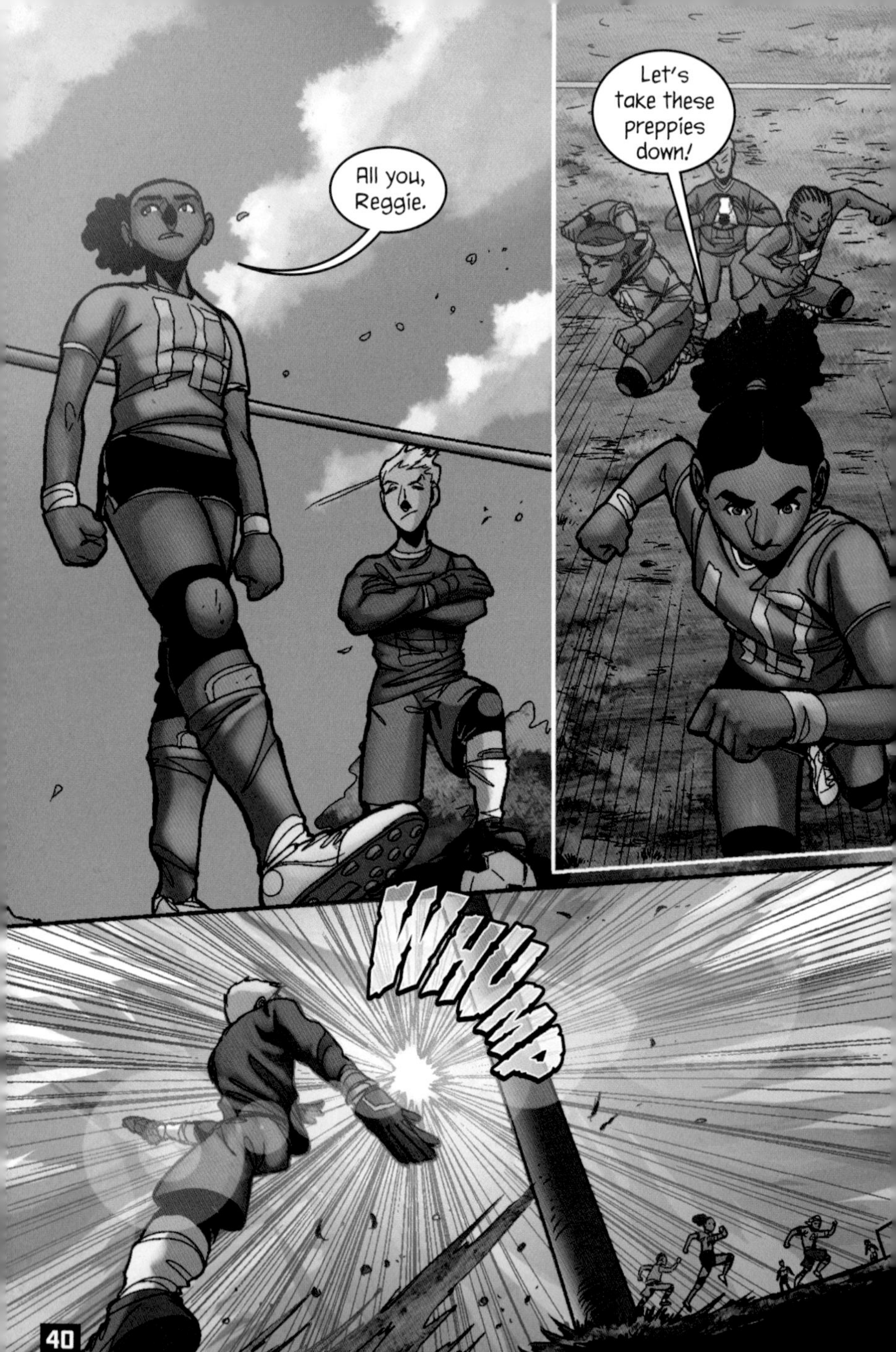
All you, Reggie.
Let's take these preppies down!
WHUMP

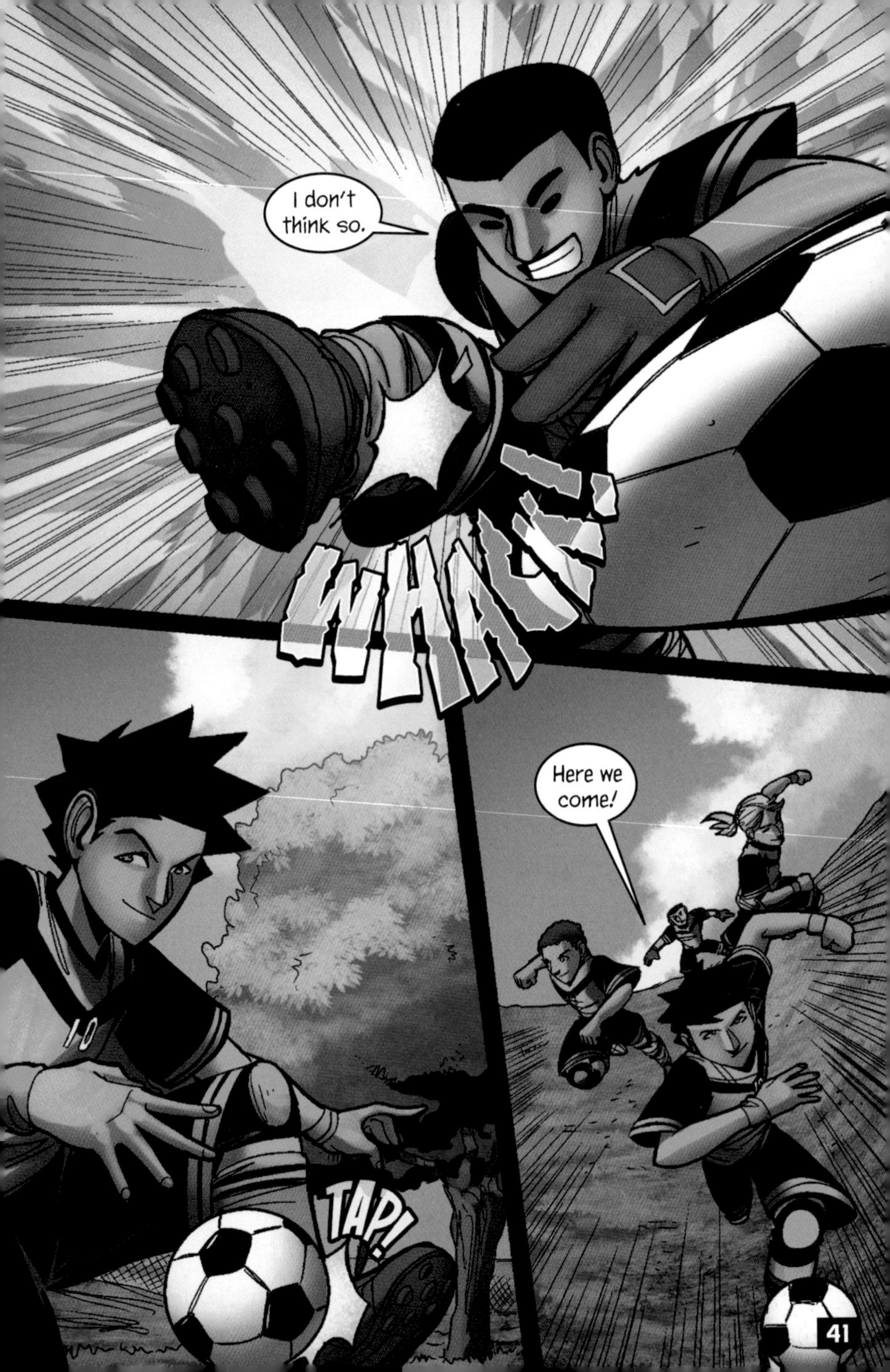
I don't think so.
WHAC!
TAP!
Here we come!

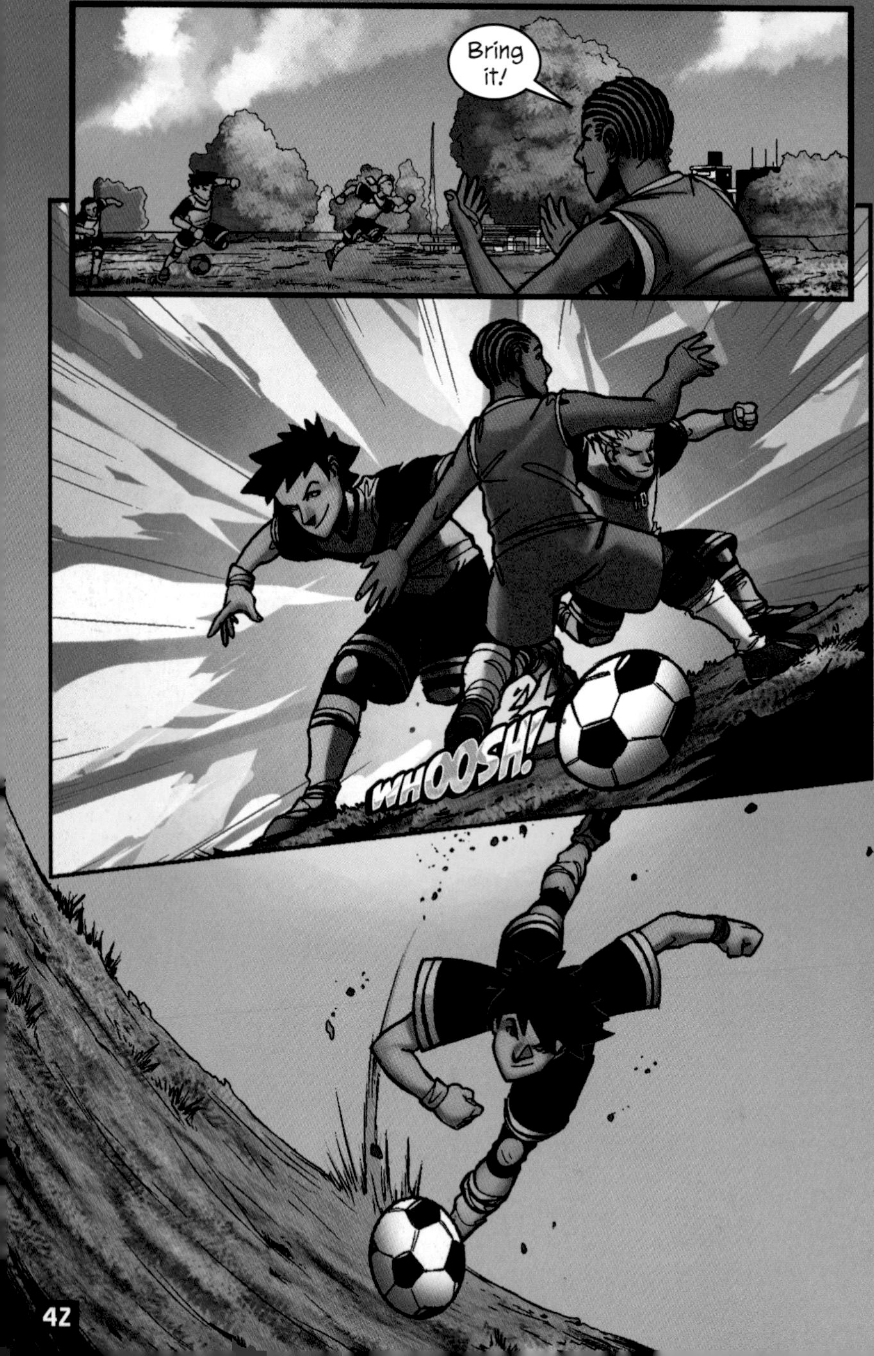

Bring it!
WHOOSH!

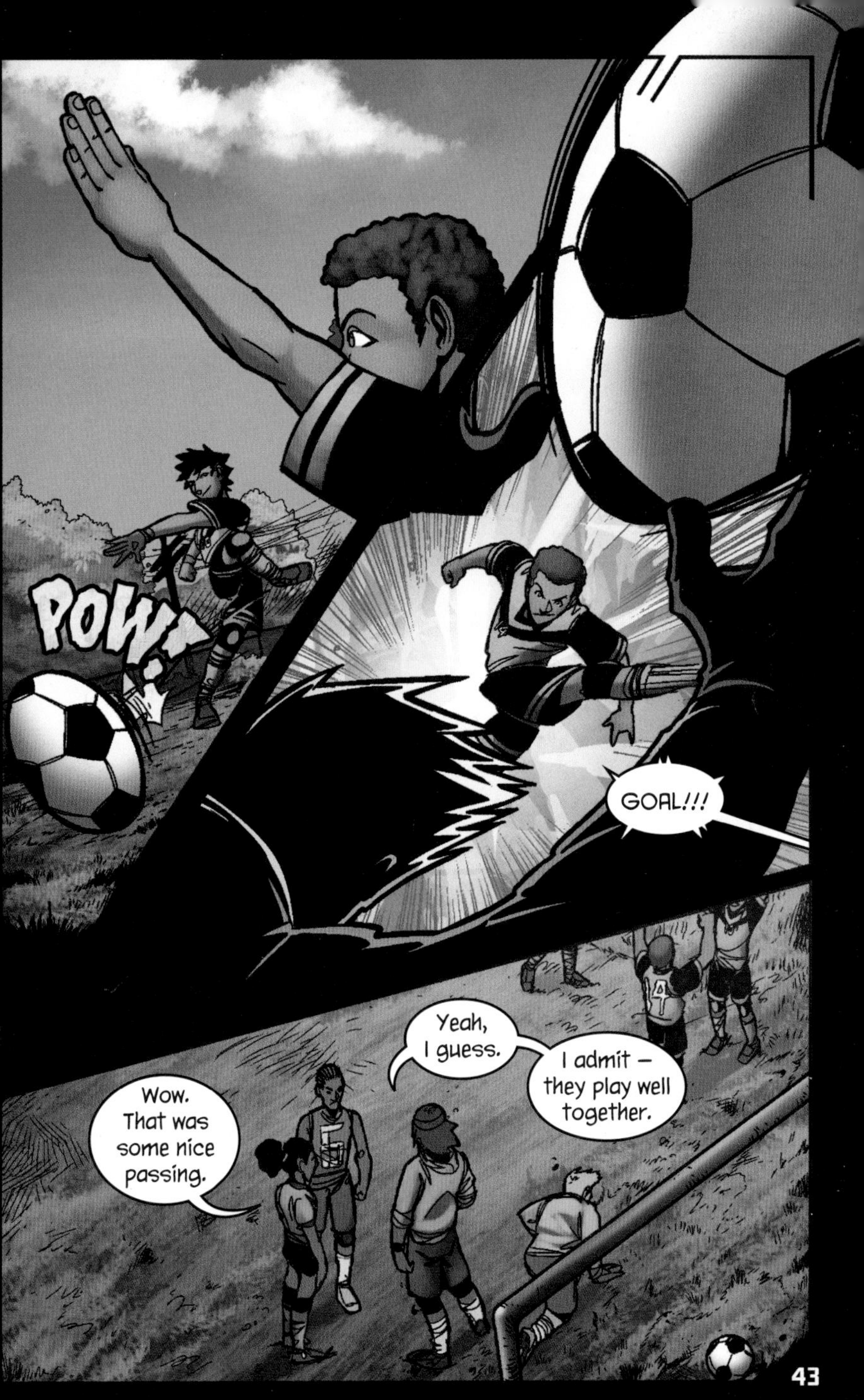
POW!
GOAL!!!
Wow. That was some nice passing.
Yeah, I guess.
I admit — they play well together.

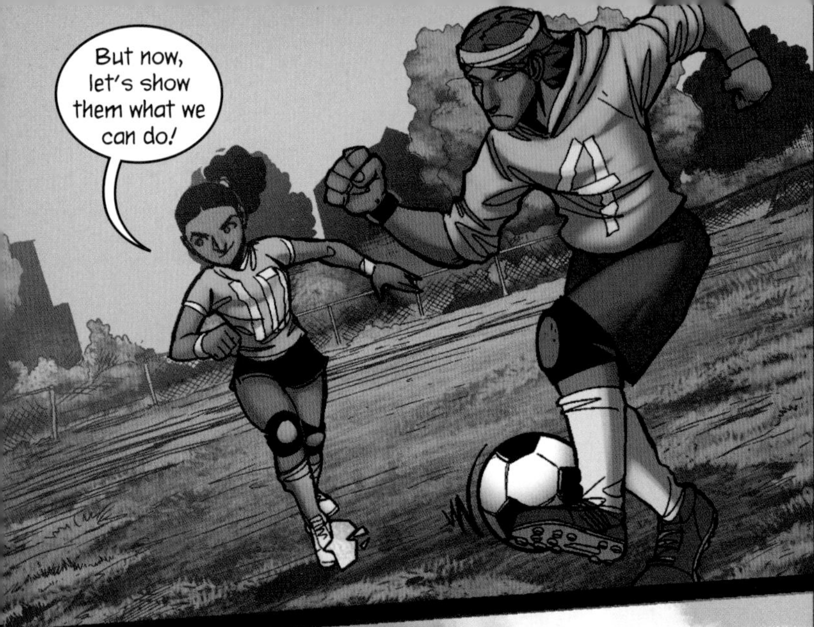
But now, let's show them what we can do!
WUMP!

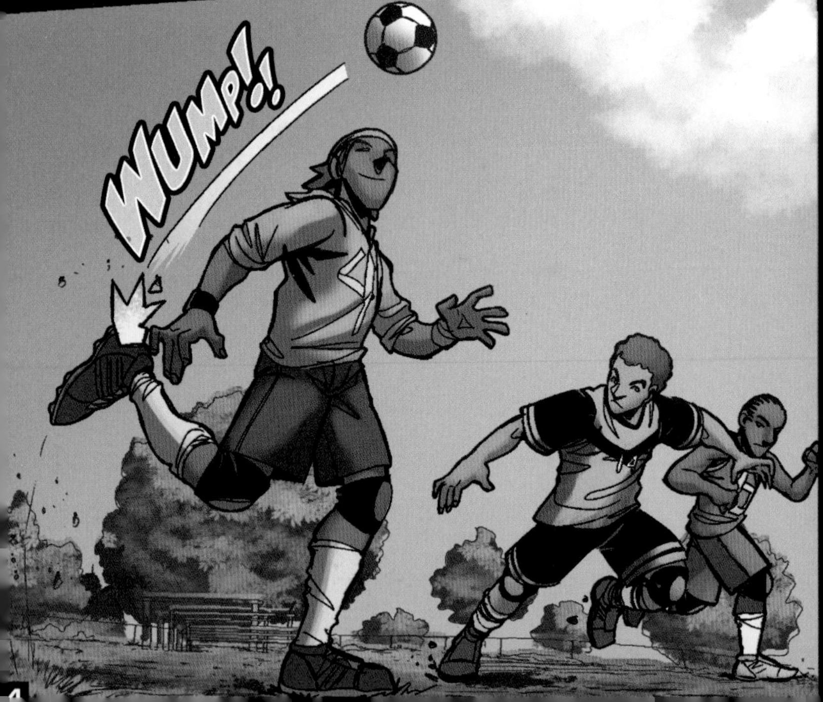

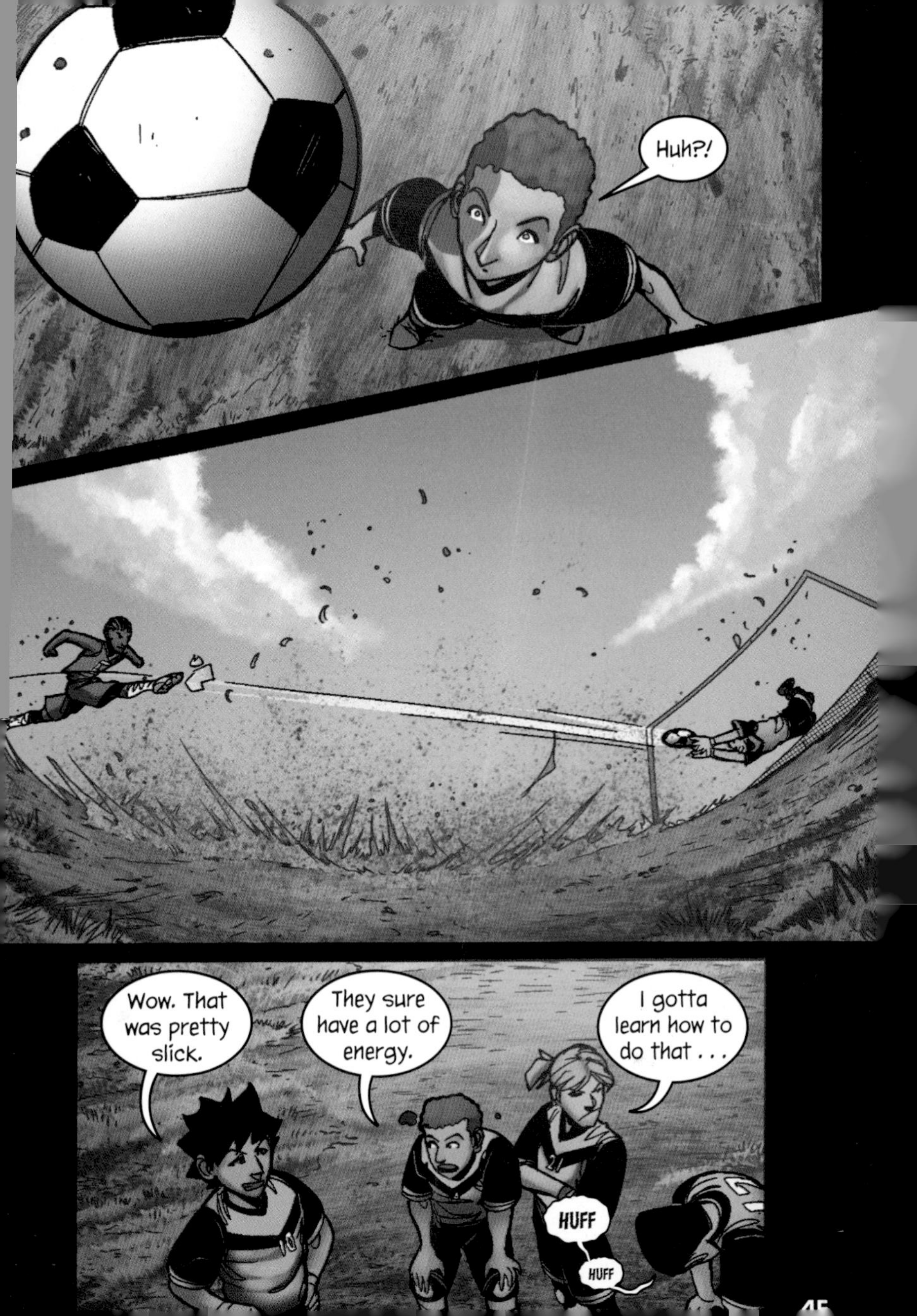
Huh?!
Wow. That was pretty slick.
They sure have a lot of energy.
I gotta learn how to do that . . .
HUFF
HUFF

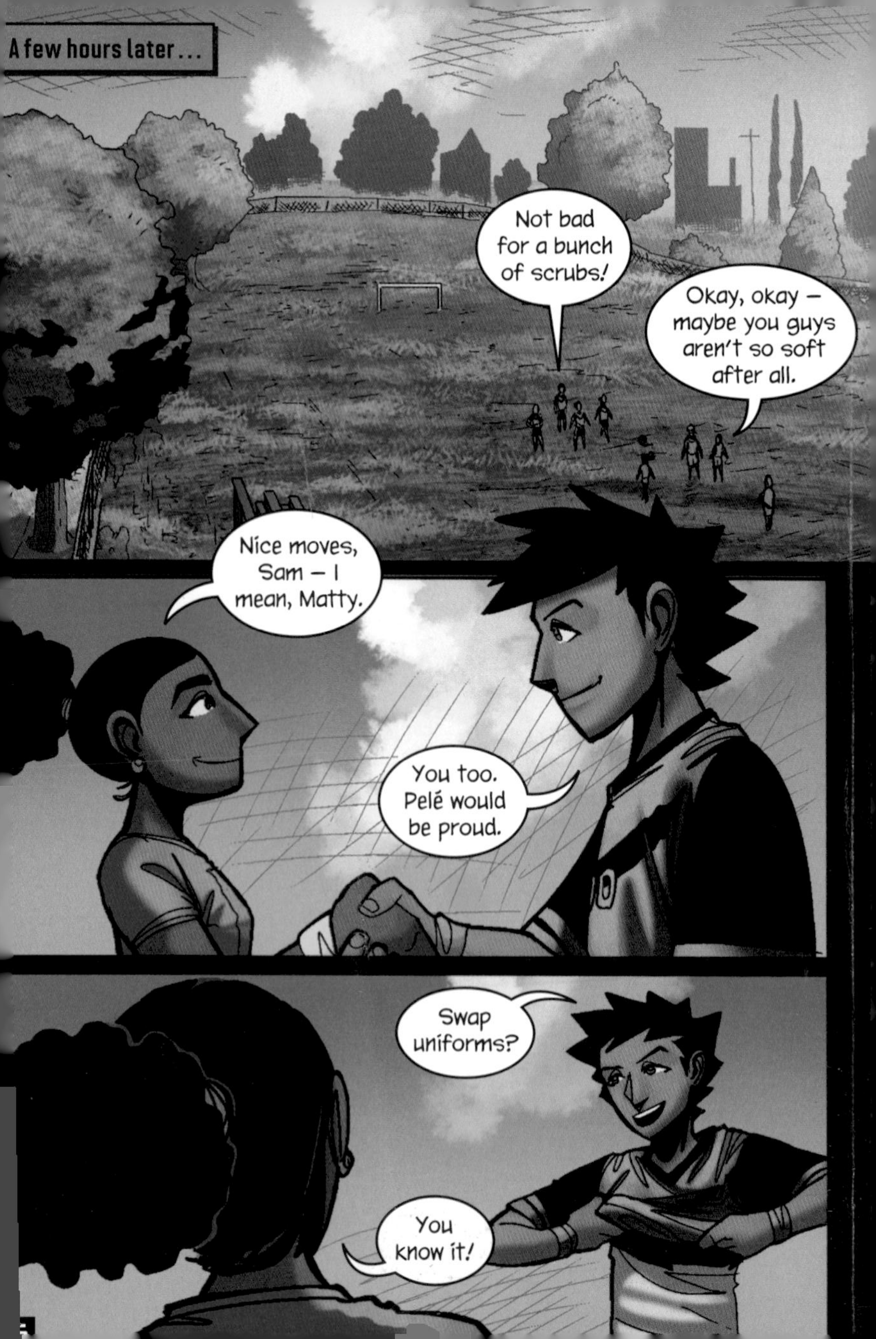
A few hours later . . .
Not bad for a bunch of scrubs!
Okay, okay — maybe you guys aren't so soft after all.
Nice moves, Sam — I mean, Matty.
You too. Pelé would be proud.
Swap uniforms?
You know it!

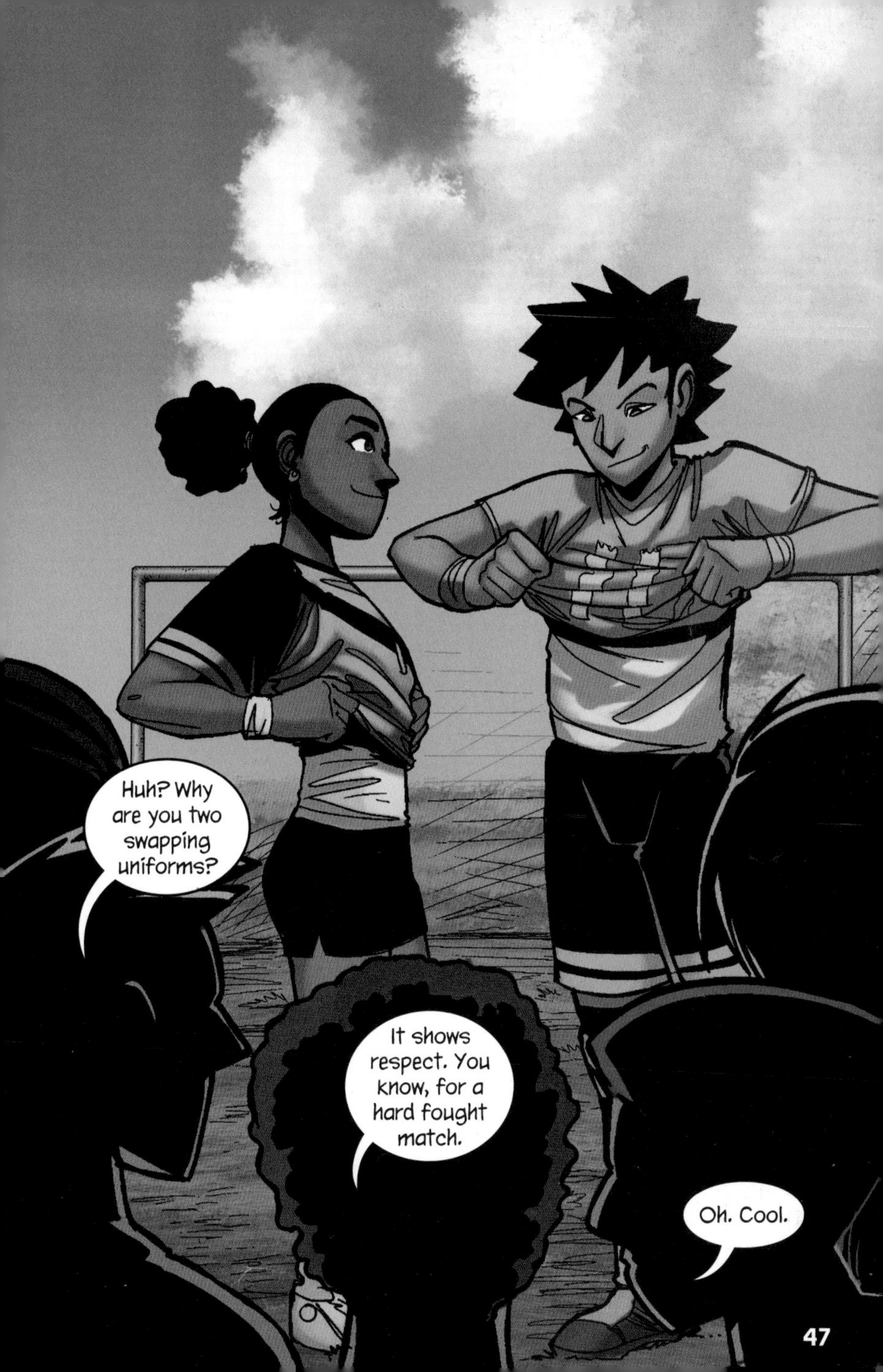
Huh? Why are you two swapping uniforms?
It shows respect. You know, for a hard fought match.
Oh. Cool.

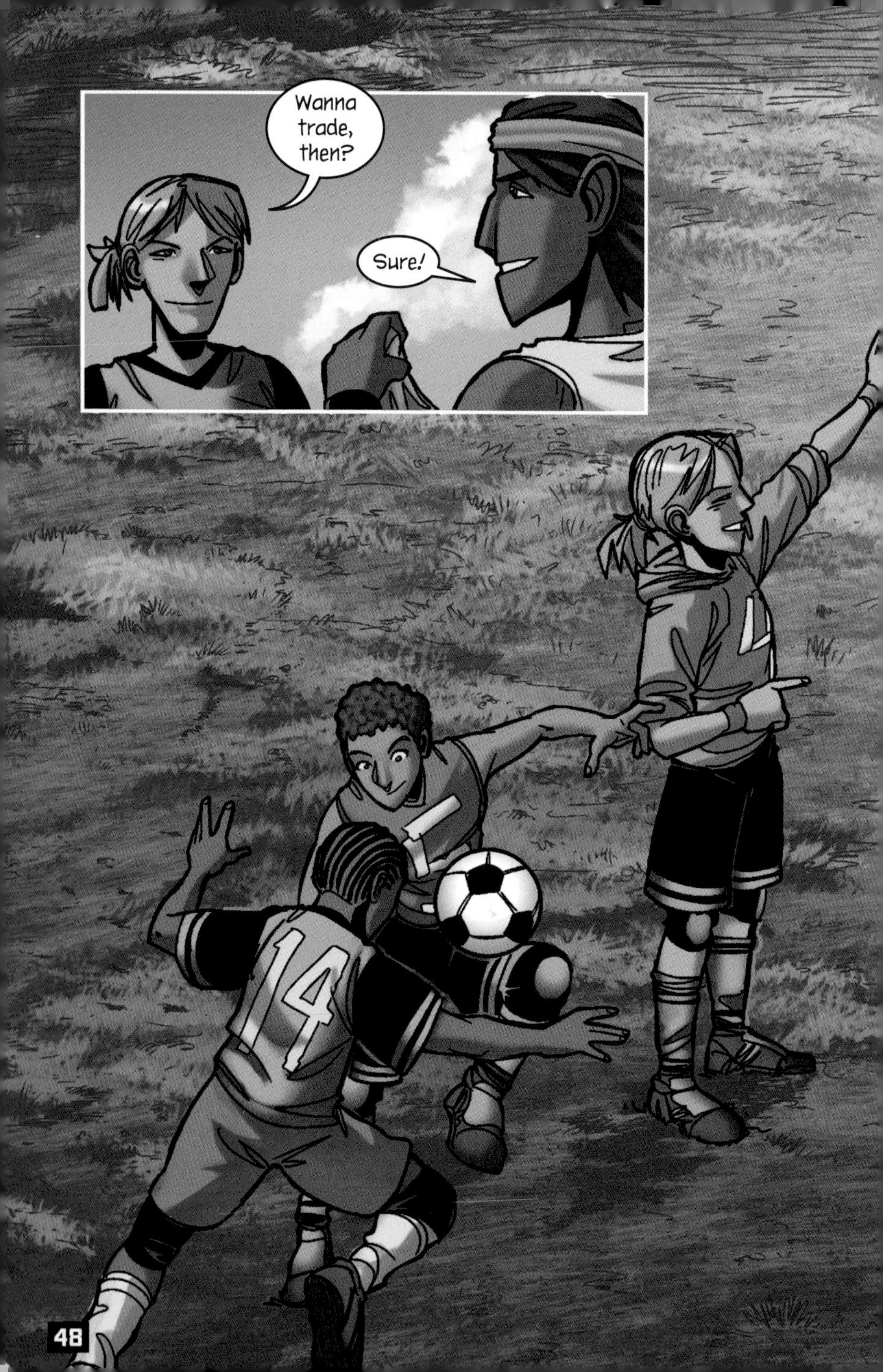
Wanna trade, then?
Sure!

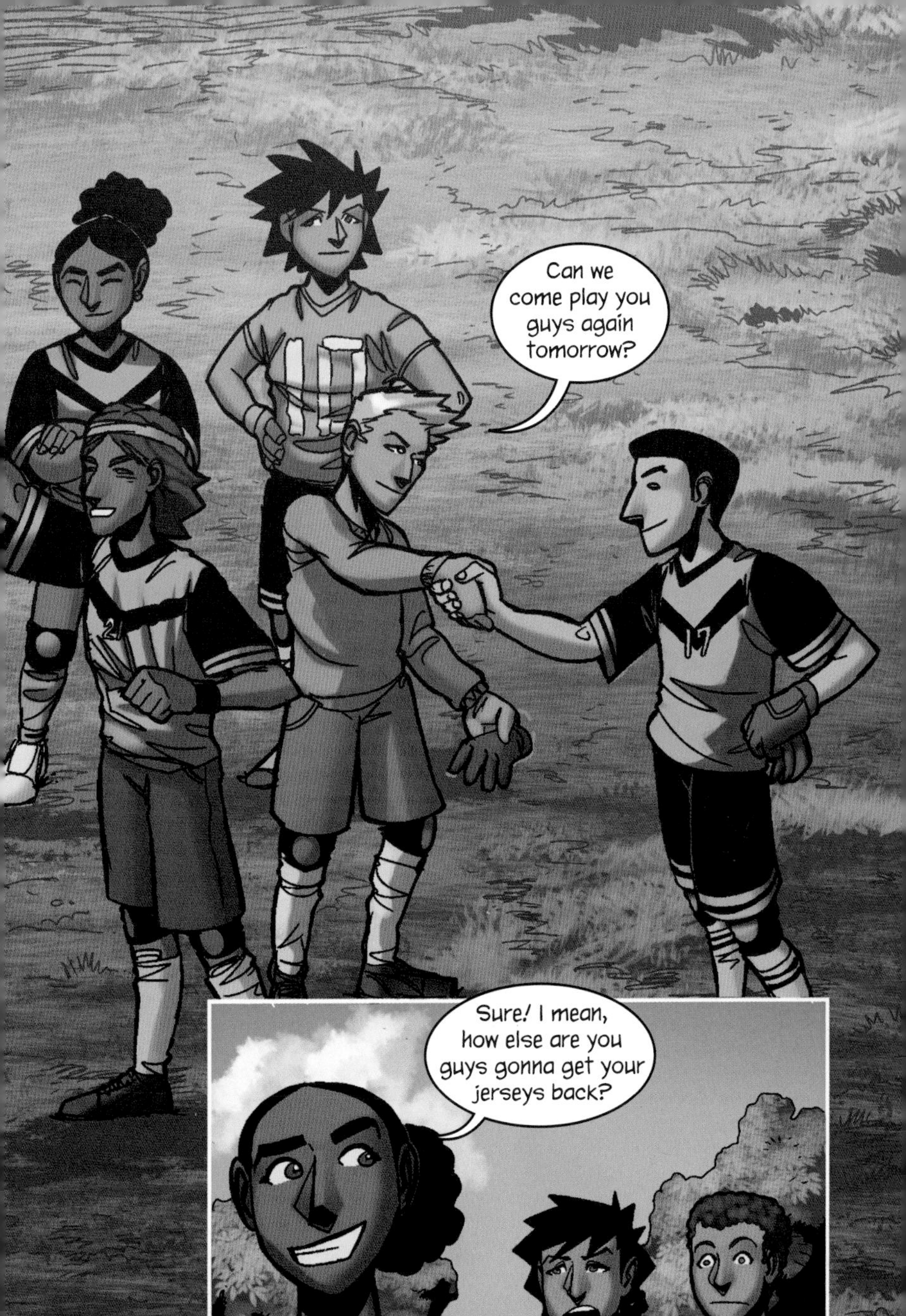
Can we come play you guys again tomorrow?
Sure! I mean, how else are you guys gonna get your jerseys back?

SPORTS ZONE
POSTGAME RECAP

SOC
SOCCER

STREETBALLERS AND STRIKERS SWAP JERSEYS, SHOW RESPECT

BY THE NUMBERS

STATS LEADERS:
ASSISTS: DIEGO, 3
GOALS: MATTY, 2

STORY: Tensions ran high between Matty and Lola's squads. Just when a backyard brawl seemed inevitable, Matty and Lola hatched a plan that led to a spirited soccer showdown between both squads. After the game, to show respect for a hard-fought soccer battle, the squads swapped jerseys with each other. Matty said, "It just goes to show that it doesn't matter *where* you play soccer — it's *how* you play that counts."

Sports Illustrated KIDS

UP NEXT: SI KIDS INFO CENTER

SZ POSTGAME EXTRA

WHERE **YOU** ANALYZE THE GAME!

BLZ vs BNS
3-1
TGR vs ROR
33-32
EAG vs BAN
14-7
SPA vs WLD
4-3
BAN vs ROR
21-15
ROR vs LIG
4-3
BLZ vs BNS

> Soccer fans got a real treat today when the streetball kids faced off against the Strikers in a flashy backyard battle. Let's go ask some fans for their thoughts on the day's big show...

DISCUSSION QUESTION 1

Matty tricked Lola and her friends. Is it okay to trick other people if you mean well? Why or why not?

DISCUSSION QUESTION 2

Matty always wants to improve his skills. What are some other ways Matty could have gotten better at playing soccer?

WRITING PROMPT 1

Who do you have more in common with — Matty or Lola? What about your life or personality makes you similar or different? Write about it.

WRITING PROMPT 2

Which soccer position is the most challenging to play? What skills do you need to play that position effectively? Write about it.

Sports Illustrated KIDS

INFO CENTER

GLOSSARY

BICYCLE KICK (BYE-si-kuhl KIK)—to perform a bicycle kick, you kick the ball over your head in mid-air while facing away from the net

CAUTIOUS (KAW-shuhss)—if you are cautious, you are being careful or trying to avoid mistakes or danger

IMPRESSED (im-PRESSD)—made people think highly of you

PROUD (PROUD)—pleased and satisfied with something

RECOGNIZE (REK-uhg-nize)—to see someone and know who the person is

RESPECT (ri-SPEKT)—to admire or have a high opinion of

STRIKER (STRIKE-ur)—a forward on a soccer team who focuses on scoring goals

STYLE (STILE)—the way in which something is done

CREATORS

C.J. Renner › Author

As well as loving to read novels, read comics, see movies, and attend galleries, C.J. Renner loves to write novels, write comics, make movies, and exhibit his visual art. He lives in his favorite city in the world, Minneapolis, where he cheers on the Twins, Vikings, and Timberwolves.

Aburtov › Penciler

Aburtov has worked in the comic book industry for more than 11 years. In that time, he has illustrated popular characters like Wolverine, Iron Man, Blade, and the Punisher. Recently, Aburtov started his own illustration studio called Graphikslava. He lives in Monterrey, Mexico, with his daughter, Ilka, and his beloved wife. Aburtov enjoys spending his spare time with family and friends.

Andres Esparza › Inker

Andres Esparza has been a graphic designer, colorist, and illustrator for many different companies and agencies. Andres now works as a full-time artist for Graphikslava studio in Monterrey, Mexico. In his spare time, Andres loves to play basketball, hang out with family and friends, and listen to good music.

Fernando Cano › Colorist

Fernando Cano is an up-and-coming illustrator living in Monterrey, Mexico. He works as a full-time illustrator and colorist at Graphikslava studio. He has done illustration work for Marvel, DC Comics, and role-playing games like Pathfinder. In his spare time, he enjoys hanging out with friends, singing, rowing, and drawing!

Sports Illustrated KIDS GRAPHIC NOVELS
QUICK COMIC

CARLOS RAMIREZ IN:
SPOTLIGHT STRIKER

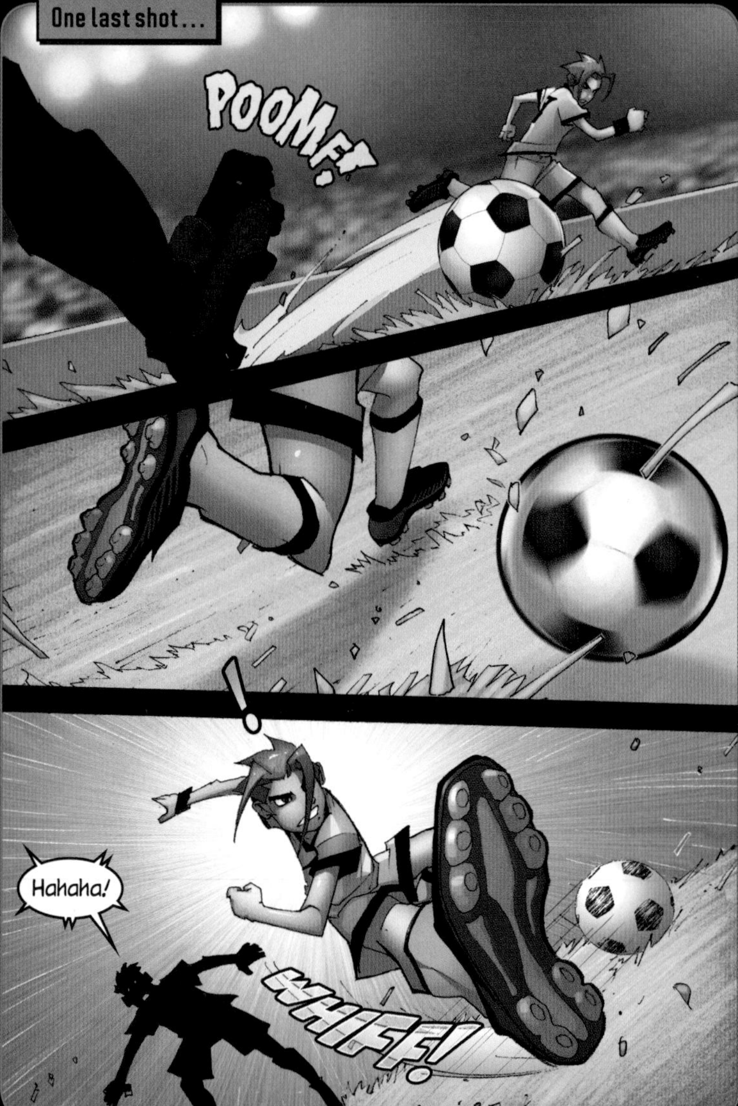

One last shot...
POOMF!
!
Hahaha!
WHIFF!

›› LOVE THIS QUICK COMIC? READ THE WHOLE STORY IN SPOTLIGHT STRIKER – ONLY FROM STONE ARCH BOOKS!

HOT SPORTS. **HOT** FORMAT!

GREAT CHARACTERS BATTLE FOR SPORTS GLORY IN TODAY'S HOTTEST FORMAT—GRAPHIC NOVELS!

THE FUN DOESN'T STOP HERE!

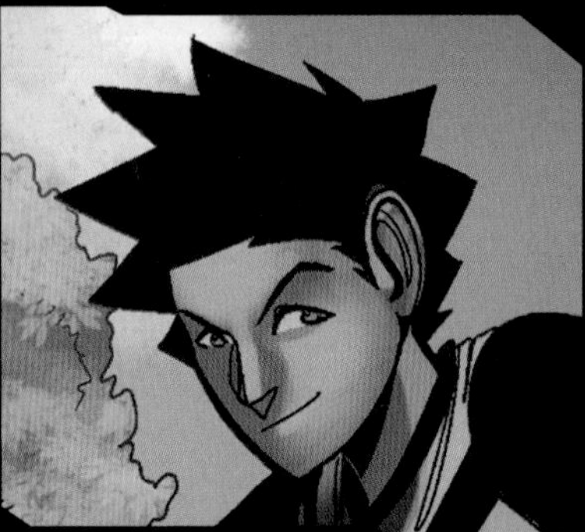

FIND MORE:
GAMES
PUZZLES
CHARACTERS

www.capstonekids.com

Still want MORE? Find cool websites and more books like this one at www.Facthound.com. Just type in the Book ID: 9781434222411 and you're ready to go!

AND FOR SPORTS HEADLINES, SCORES, STATS, PHOTOS, COOL GAMES . . . SIKIDS.COM

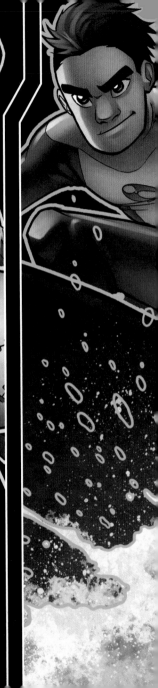

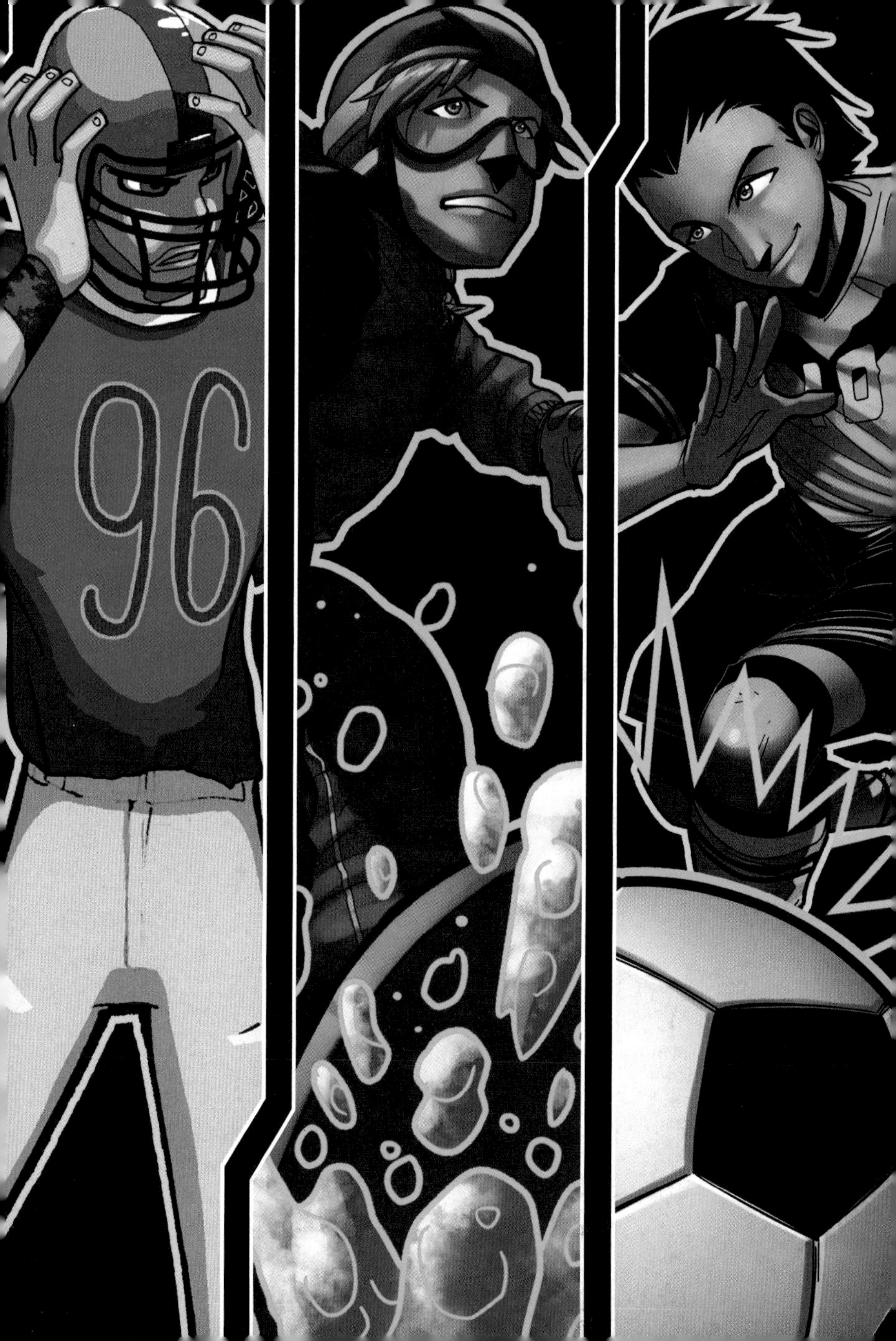

Sports Illustrated KIDS

GRAPHIC NOVELS

STONE ARCH BOOKS
a capstone imprint